Copyright©2023 Ertugrul Od

Revenge Stories
by Ertugrul Odabasi

Alice

Alice had always been the target of bullying. From a young age, she was teased for being overweight and unattractive, and it only got worse as she grew older. In high school, she was the butt of every joke and felt like she had no escape from the constant torment.

"I don't understand why they do it," Alice said to her mother one day. "What did I ever do to them?"

"I don't know, honey," her mother replied, hugging her. "People can be cruel sometimes. But remember that you're beautiful and special in your way."

At first, Alice tried to ignore the teasing and rise above it. She focused on her studies and hobbies, hoping the bullies would eventually leave her alone. But as time went on, the abuse only got worse.

One day, as Alice was walking home from school, a group of boys started taunting her. "Hey, fatty!" one of them yelled. "Why don't you eat a salad instead of a Big Mac?"

Alice tried to keep walking, but the boys followed her. "What's the matter, can't take a joke?" another one said, laughing.

Finally, Alice had enough. She turned around and faced the boys. "You know what? I'm sick of this. I'm sick of you guys making fun of me all the time. Why don't you leave me alone?"

The boys laughed and walked away, but Alice felt satisfied that she had stood up for herself.

Over time, Alice started to take control of her own life. She began to work out, eat healthier, and lose weight. She also started dressing better, wearing makeup, and feeling more confident.

At first, the change in her appearance was met with surprise and even admiration. But the teasing became more sinister as Alice blossomed into a beautiful, confident young woman.

One day, Alice was walking home from the grocery store and saw a group of her former bullies across the street. They laughed and pointed in her direction, and Alice could feel her heart racing.

"Hey, Alice!" one of them yelled. "Looking good, girl!"

Alice could feel her face turning red with anger. "What do you want?" she yelled back.

"Nothing just wanted to say hi to an old friend," another one said, grinning.

Alice knew that they were up to something, and she braced herself for the worst.

Over the next few weeks, the bullying continued. Former bullies spread rumors about her, sabotaged her relationships, and even physically assaulted her. Alice tried to ignore and rise above the abuse, but she couldn't escape the constant reminders of her past.

One day, Alice couldn't take it anymore. She snapped and decided to get revenge on those who had hurt her. She spent weeks planning and executing a series of elaborate pranks, each more vicious than the last.

"I'm sick of being the victim," Alice said to herself as she set up a hidden camera to catch one of her former bullies in the act. "It's time for them to feel the same pain and humiliation I've felt for many years."

She felt a sense of satisfaction as she watched the footage of her former bully falling into a mud pit that Alice had set up. "That's what you get," she said, laughing.

But as Alice continued down this path of revenge, she began to realize that she was becoming the bully. Alice realized she was becoming the bully as she continued this revenge path. She was no better than those who had tormented her in the past.

She tried to stop, but the anger and hatred inside her were too powerful. She sought revenge, taking it out on anyone who had ever wronged her, whether they deserved it or not.

As Alice's pranks became more and more elaborate, she began to lose touch with reality. Her desire for revenge consumed her, and it was starting to take a toll on her mental health.

One day, Alice's mother received a call from the police. They had arrested Alice for vandalism and destruction of property. Her mother was shocked and devastated.

"I don't understand," she said to the police officer. "What could have driven her to do something like this?"

The police officer sighed. "We believe your daughter was seeking revenge on someone who hurt her. It's a sad situation, but we've seen it happen."

Alice's mother was heartbroken. She had always known that her daughter had been the victim of bullying, but she never thought that it would lead to something like this.

Alice was sent to a mental health facility, receiving therapy and treatment for her anger and aggression. It was a long and challenging journey, but she eventually began to heal.

As Alice worked through her issues, she realized that revenge was not the answer. It only led to more pain and suffering for herself and those around her.

She focused on forgiveness and empathy, reaching out to those she had hurt and apologizing for her actions. It was a challenging and humbling experience, but she needed to move on and find peace.

Years later, Alice was able to rebuild her life. She went back to school and got a degree in psychology, intending to help others who had been through similar experiences.

She also advocated for anti-bullying and mental health awareness, sharing her story with others and working to prevent others from going down the same dark path she had gone down.

Ultimately, Alice found redemption and healing, but it came at a high cost. She had to confront her demons and face the pain and trauma of her past.

But through it all, she learned that forgiveness and empathy were the keys to a happy and fulfilling life. And that sometimes, the greatest revenge is simply living well.

The Revenge of the Camel

The caravan led by Omar had been traveling through the barren Arabian desert for weeks. They had already crossed miles of dunes and were running low on supplies. Water was scarce, and their camels were growing tired and irritable.

As the sun set, the caravan stopped at a small oasis. The travelers were grateful for the chance to rest and replenish their supplies. Omar had led the fleet for over 30 years and knew how to navigate the desert. He was a wise older man who commanded the respect of his fellow travelers.

While the others were setting up camp, Omar checked on his camel, Hassan. Hassan had been Omar's faithful companion for over a decade and was like family to him. But when Omar reached Hassan's enclosure, he found that the camel had been brutally slaughtered.

Omar was devastated by the loss of his beloved camel. He knew the desert had many dangers but never thought someone would harm his companion. He swore to find the culprit and pay them for their actions.

As the days passed, Omar searched for clues and asked travelers if they had seen or heard anything suspicious. He eventually heard rumors of a group of bandits who had been attacking caravans and stealing their supplies. It was said that they were led by a ruthless man named Malik.

Omar knew he had to find Malik and pay him for his actions. He embarked on a dangerous journey through the desert, hoping to find the bandit's hideout.

As he traveled, he encountered a group of Bedouins known for their sword skill. They were a nomadic tribe that lived in the desert and were feared by many. Omar convinced the Bedouins to help him in his quest for revenge, promising them a large sum of money if they helped him defeat Malik and his army.

Omar and the Bedouins traveled for days until they finally came across a small village they believed was the bandit's headquarters. They disguised themselves as travelers and started to gather information.

One night, while resting in a tavern, they overheard Malik and his men boasting about their latest attack on a caravan. They laughed and joked about the loot they had stolen, including a valuable ruby from a wealthy trader.

Omar knew that this was his chance to strike. He signaled to the Bedouins, and they made their way to the bandit's hideout. They launched a surprise attack on the bandits, catching them off guard.

The battle was fierce, and many lives were lost. However, Omar and the Bedouins emerged victorious. They captured Malik and his followers and brought them to justice.

As they returned to the village, Omar realized that his revenge had come at a high cost. He had lost many friends and companions on the journey and knew he could never bring back his beloved camel, Hassan.

While contemplating his losses, Omar noticed a strange figure watching them. The figure was wearing a hooded cloak, and his face was obscured. Omar could feel a sense of unease emanating from the constitution, and he wondered if it was a sign of something ominous.

The figure disappeared as suddenly as he had appeared, leaving Omar with a deep sense of foreboding. He realized his quest for revenge only led to more pain and suffering. He vowed never to seek revenge again and live a peaceful and forgiving life.

And so, Omar and the Bedouins continued their journey through the desert, carrying the lessons they had learned on their quest for revenge. They knew the desert was harsh and unforgiving but beautiful and wonderful.

Omar realized that his camel, Hassan, had taught him many valuable lessons. He had taught him the importance of loyalty and companionship, and he had shown him the beauty of the desert. He knew that he would always cherish the memories he had of his beloved companion.

As they traveled, the group encountered many challenges and obstacles. They had to face dangerous sandstorms, scorching heat, and treacherous terrain. But they also experienced moments of great beauty, like a magnificent sunset over the dunes or a desert bird singing in the distance.

Eventually, they reached their destination, a bustling city on the edge of the desert. The town starkly contrasted with the barren landscape they had been traveling through. It was filled with people from all over the world and a hub of trade and commerce.

Omar and the Bedouins stayed in the city for a few days, resting and recuperating from their journey. They explored the markets and bazaars, sampling exotic foods and spices. They also met many interesting people, including a wise old merchant who shared his knowledge of the desert with them.

While preparing to leave the city, Omar noticed the hooded figure again. This time, he was standing in the shadows of an alleyway, watching them. Omar felt a chill run down his spine as he realized the figure had followed them all along.

He decided to confront the figure and made his way toward the alleyway. As he got closer, the figure stepped out of the shadows, revealing himself as an older man with a long white beard.

The older man spoke in a voice that was barely above a whisper. "I have been watching you, Omar. Your quest for revenge has led you down a dangerous path. But you have learned an important lesson, and you must now use that knowledge to help others."

The older man's words took Omar aback. He realized that the man was right. His quest for revenge had consumed him, and he had lost sight of what was truly important.

The older man continued. "You must use your experiences to help others lost and wandering in the desert. You must show them the way and help them find their path."

Omar nodded, understanding the older man's message. He knew that he had to use his experiences to help others. He thanked the older man and returned to the caravan, ready to embark on a new journey.

As they set out into the desert once again, Omar felt a sense of peace and contentment. He knew he had learned a valuable lesson and was ready to share his knowledge with others. And he was prepared to explore it with a renewed sense of purpose and wonder.

The Bedouin caravan continued their journey through the desert, guided by Omar's newfound wisdom and a sense of purpose. They encountered many lost and wandering travelers, and Omar was always willing to lend a hand and help them find their way.

As they traveled, Omar was drawn to the desert's more mysterious and mystical aspects. He learned from the Bedouin elders about the ancient traditions and beliefs the desert nomads still hold dear. He listened to stories of powerful djinns and jinnis who roamed the desert sands and hidden oases where magic lingered.

One night, as they camped in the desert, Omar had a vivid dream. In the dream, he was visited by a beautiful woman who spoke to him in a language he didn't understand. She seemed to be trying to tell him something, but he couldn't make out her words.

The following day, Omar described the dream to the Bedouin elders. They listened carefully and then told him that the woman he had seen was likely a jinni, a powerful spirit that was said to inhabit the desert. They noted that the jinni had probably been trying to communicate with him and that he should look for signs and omens that might reveal her message.

As they continued their journey, Omar kept his eyes and ears open, hoping for a sign from the jinni. One day, as they passed through a particularly remote and desolate part of the desert, they came across a strange and otherworldly sight.

In the distance, they could see a group of camels grazing in a small oasis. But as they got closer, they realized the camels differed from any they had ever seen. They were tall and sleek, with coats that shimmered like gold in the sunlight. And as they watched, the camels began to glow as if a bright aura surrounded them.

The Bedouins were stunned by the sight, but Omar felt a sense of recognition. He realized that this was the sign he had been waiting for, the message from the jinni. He knew that the camels were not of this world but that they had been sent to guide him on his journey.

Without hesitation, Omar and the Bedouins followed the camels into the desert, knowing that they were being led by a force greater than themselves. They traveled for days, guided by the shimmering camels, until they came to a hidden valley deep in the heart of the desert.

A massive stone structure stood in the valley's center, unlike anything they had ever seen. It was a towering edifice of black stone with strange and intricate carvings covering its surface. A large stone door was at the structure's base, sealed shut by a massive lock.

Omar and the Bedouins approached the door, feeling a sense of awe and trepidation. They knew this place was powerful and mysterious and were treading on sacred ground.

As they stood before the door, the lock suddenly began to turn as if moved by an invisible force. The door slowly swung open, revealing a dimly lit chamber within.

Omar and the Bedouins entered the chamber without hesitation, ready to discover the secrets. They knew they were on the brink of something extraordinary that would change their lives forever.

Revenge of John

In 1999, John was a young man living in a small town with his wife and daughter. One day, while he was at work, he received a call from the police informing him that his wife had been found dead in their home. John was devastated, but he was even more shocked when he was accused of her murder. Despite his protestations of innocence, John was found guilty and sentenced to 25 years in prison.

While in prison, John had plenty of time to think and reflect on his life. He also took advantage of the prison library and read hundreds of books on various subjects, including law, philosophy, and history. He became a knowledgeable man, and his worldview changed.

After 23 long years, John was finally released from prison. As he stepped outside the prison gates, he looked around and saw a world very different from what he remembered. His family was dispersed. His wife had remarried, and his daughter, who was only a baby when he went to prison, had grown up to become a notorious criminal.

John was determined to start over but didn't know where to begin. He had no money, job, or place to stay when he met a young man named Max. Max was the son of the big boss in town, and he offered John a place to stay and a job in his father's business.

At first, John was hesitant to accept Max's offer. He knew that Max's father was a criminal, and he didn't want to get involved in any illegal activities. But as I thought about his situation. So, he accepted Max's offer and began working for the boss.

John was surprised to find that he enjoyed working for the boss. The work was challenging, and he felt like he was part of a team. He also found himself becoming good friends with Max. Max was a young man who had grown up in privilege but was also intelligent and had a good heart. The two men bonded over their love of books and philosophy.

As time passed, John realized the boss was not the ruthless criminal he had imagined. He was a man who had grown up in poverty and turned to crime to provide for his family. John began to see him as a kind of Robin Hood figure who took from the rich and gave to the poor.

One day, John was asked to handle a problem for the boss. He was told that someone had stolen a valuable piece of artwork from one of the boss's clients, and he was to find out who did it and get the painting back. John set to work, and after a few days, he found out that the person who had stolen the picture was none other than his daughter.

John was devastated to learn this but knew he had to do something. He talked to Max and told him the truth about his daughter. Max was shocked but sympathetic and helped John devise a plan to get the painting back without involving the boss.

The plan worked, and John retrieved the painting and returned it to the client. He also had a heart-to-heart talk with his daughter and convinced her to turn her life around. She agreed to leave her life of crime behind and start over.

As the days went by, John began to feel a sense of peace that he had never known before. The loss of his wife still saddened him, but he had found a new family in Max and the boss. He had also found a way to make amends for his past mistakes and to help his daughter find a better path.

In the end, John realized that he had In the end, John realized that he had been given a second chance at life. He had spent 23 years in prison but emerged a better person. He had learned to see the world in a different light, and he had found a new purpose in life.

Over the next few years, John worked hard for the boss and became one of his most trusted employees. He also reconnected with his daughter and helped her turn her life around. Together, they started a small business selling handmade crafts, which became a success.

John's relationship with Max also grew more robust over time. Max had always been fascinated by John's intelligence and knowledge, and the two of them would often have long conversations about philosophy and literature. They became close friends, and Max even offered to help John track down his wife's natural killer.

With Max's help, John was able to find new evidence that proved his innocence. The natural killer was finally caught and brought to justice. John's name was cleared, and he could eventually move on from the past.

As John looked back on his life, he realized that everything that had happened to him had led him to this moment. He had been given a second chance at life and made the most of it. He had found a new family, a new purpose, and a new sense of peace.

In the end, John knew that he had indeed been blessed. He had overcome the injustice that had been done to him and found a way to make a difference in the world. He had become a better man and knew his wife would be proud of him.

With gratitude and contentment, John looked up at the sky and whispered a prayer of thanks. He knew he had finally found the happiness and fulfillment that had eluded him for so long.

As John's life settled into a new normal, he never forgot the lessons he had learned in prison. He knew that life could be unpredictable and that the only thing he could control was how he responded to it.

He also realized that he had a unique opportunity to help others who the justice system had wronged. He began volunteering at a local nonprofit organization that provided legal assistance to those who couldn't afford it. He also advocated for prison reform, speaking out about the need for more rehabilitation and education programs within the system.

In many ways, John had become a symbol of hope for those who had lost their way. His story inspired many, and his dedication to making a difference in the world was a reminder that it's never too late to change your life.

As the years passed, John watched as his daughter grew into a successful businesswoman and his granddaughter began college. He remained close with Max, who had become a successful writer and continued to use his platform to advocate for justice.

As for John himself, he lived a long and fulfilling life, surrounded by the love and respect of those he had helped along the way. When he passed away, he left a legacy of resilience, perseverance, and compassion that would continue to inspire generations.

And so, the story of John came to a close. But his spirit lived on in the hearts of those his remarkable journey had touched.

Hostage

As the sun rose on the sixth day of the standoff, Ahmed made a decision. He released Jack, and the two men walked out of the small room together. They faced the world side by side, with the media capturing every moment.

"Thank you," Jack said, his voice choked with emotion.

Ahmed looked at him, his eyes filled with anger and sadness. "Don't thank me," he said. "I did what I had to do."

Jack nodded, understanding. "I know. But still, I'm grateful."

They stood in silence for a moment before Ahmed spoke again. "I want you to know that I don't hate Americans. I don't hate you."

"I know," Jack said. "I don't hate Iraqis either. I never wanted to be here. I never wanted any of this to happen."

Ahmed nodded. "I understand. But my people have suffered, and I couldn't stand by and do nothing. I had to make a statement."

Jack looked at him, trying to find the words to express his feelings. "I get that. But violence isn't the answer. It only leads to more suffering."

Ahmed sighed. "I know. But sometimes it feels like there's no other way."

They continued to talk to share their stories and their perspectives. In the following days and weeks, they found a way to connect and see each other as fellow human beings rather than enemies.

The ordeal was over for Jack and his family, but the scars remained. They returned home to the States, forever changed by the experience. They had seen humanity's best and worst and knew the world was more complex and dangerous than they had ever imagined.

As for Ahmed, his quest for justice continued. He knew his grandfather's death could never be undone, but he was determined to ensure his story was never forgotten. He continued to speak out, fight for his beliefs, and make his voice heard. And in the end, that was all that anyone could do. Over time, the media coverage of the event died down, and Jack and Ahmed returned to their daily lives. However, the experience stayed with them, haunting them in their ways.

Jack became a vocal advocate for better mental health resources for returning soldiers. He used his experience as a hostage to shed light on the realities of PTSD and trauma. He spoke at conferences and wrote articles, hoping to make a difference in the lives of others who had been through similar experiences.

Ahmed, on the other hand, continued to fight for his cause. He wrote a book about his experience, translated into multiple languages, bringing his story to people worldwide. He became a symbol of the resistance against the occupation of Iraq and used his platform to speak out against the injustices he saw around him.

Years passed, and both men grew old. But their memories of that time remained vivid, etched into their minds like scars that would never fade. Even as the world continued to change, they carried the weight of their experiences with them, knowing they had been a part of something that would never be forgotten.

Stories like this reminded us of the importance of empathy, compassion, and understanding as the world grappled with the legacy of the Iraq War and the ongoing challenges of global conflict and violence. They showed us that there was always hope for healing and reconciliation, even amid the most complex and painful circumstances.

For Jack and Ahmed, the experience had been a turning point, a moment of reckoning that had changed their lives. They had been forced to confront the reality of war, to see the human cost of conflict up close, and to grapple with their own moral and ethical convictions.

But in the end, they emerged from the experience more robust, wiser, and more compassionate than ever. And they knew that, no matter what the future held, they would always carry the lessons they had learned as a reminder of the power of human connection and the potential for healing and hope, even in the darkest times.

The Perfect Plan

As James walked home from work, his mind was consumed with thoughts of revenge. His boss had wronged him, and Mr. Johnson had stolen a promotion from him that was rightfully his. James had been planning his revenge for weeks and was sure he had the perfect plan to bring Mr. Johnson down.

James spent countless hours researching, gathering evidence, and preparing for his revenge plot. He was meticulous and thorough, leaving no stone unturned in his pursuit of justice. He even took the time to rehearse his lines and practice his acting to ensure that his plan would go off without a hitch.

The day of reckoning finally arrived, and James put his plan into action. He approached Mr. Johnson in his office, confronting him with all the evidence he had gathered against him. Mr. Johnson was caught off guard, and James felt a rush of satisfaction as he watched the fear in his boss's eyes.

But as the conversation continued, something began to feel off. Mr. Johnson's responses seemed genuine, and James started questioning whether he had made a mistake. Suddenly, the door to the office burst open, and James's coworker, Rachel, entered the room.

"James, you have to stop this," Rachel said urgently. "Mr. Johnson is innocent. The real culprit is someone else."

James was stunned. He had been so convinced that he was doing the right thing that he had never even considered the possibility of being wrong. Rachel went on to explain that the real culprit was someone who had been working with James all along, someone who had been feeding him false information and leading him down the wrong path.

James was shaken to his core. He had been so consumed with his desire for revenge that he had let his anger close his eyes to the truth.

At that moment, he realized he had been the villain and hurt innocent people in his quest for justice.

As James sat in the office, contemplating the consequences of his actions, he knew he had a long road ahead to make things right. But he was determined to do so, to make amends and seek forgiveness from those he had wronged. And he knew that he had learned a valuable lesson about the dangers of revenge and the importance of seeing the world clearly, even when it's not what we want to see.

James left Mr. Johnson's office feeling shaken and confused. He couldn't believe that he had been so blind to the truth and that he had hurt innocent people in his quest for revenge. He knew he had a lot of work to do to make things right, but he was determined to do so.

Over the next few days, James reached out to everyone he had hurt, apologizing for his actions and trying to make amends. He was surprised that most people were willing to forgive him, and he felt a sense of relief and gratitude for their kindness.

But there was still one person who he needed to make things right with- the actual victim of his revenge plot. He knew that he had hurt them deeply and that they might not be willing to forgive him.

One day, James gathered the courage to visit the person's home. His heart was pounding with nervousness and anxiety as he knocked on the door. When the door opened, he was met with a cold and distant gaze from the person he had wronged.

"I know I hurt you, and I'm so sorry," James began. "My anger and desire for revenge blinded me, and I didn't see the truth until it was too late. But I want to make it right. I want to do whatever I can to make things better."

The person looked at James for a long moment and then let out a long sigh. "I don't know if I can forgive you," they said. "But I can see that you're sincere in your apology, and I appreciate that. I need time to think about things, but maybe we can move forward one day."

James felt a wave of relief and gratitude wash over him. He knew it wouldn't be easy to repair the damage he had done, but he was willing to do whatever it took to make things right.

James felt a sense of hope and renewal as he walked away from the person's home. He knew that he had a lot of work to do to make things right, but he had learned a valuable lesson about the dangers of revenge and the importance of seeking the truth, even when it's hard to see.

In the following days, James worked hard to prove he was a changed person. He began volunteering at a local charity organization and taking anger management classes. He even contacted Mr. Johnson, his former boss, and apologized for his wrongful accusations.

To his surprise, Mr. Johnson was gracious and forgiving. He understood that James had been acting out of anger and desperation and was happy to put the incident behind them. James felt a sense of relief and gratitude for Mr. Johnson's kindness and knew he had been given a second chance to make things right.

James continued to work hard as time passed to be a better person. He focused on being kind, honest, and compassionate and tried to live his life in a way that would make amends for his past mistakes.

And eventually, the person he had wronged reached out to him. They told him that they had seen the changes he had made and that they were willing to forgive him. James felt a sense of relief and gratitude wash over him, and he knew he had been given a second chance at life.

Ultimately, James realized that seeking revenge had only led him down a dark path. But he also knew it had taught him a valuable lesson about the importance of forgiveness and redemption. He vowed never to let his anger and desire for revenge get the best of him again and always strive to improve.

And as he looked back on his journey, he knew he had become stronger and more resilient than ever. With a newfound sense of purpose, James dedicated his life to helping others. He started a nonprofit organization that provided support and resources to people who had been wronged. He used his own experiences to teach them the dangers of revenge and the importance of forgiveness.

As he looked out at the people he had helped, James felt a sense of pride and satisfaction that he had never experienced before. He knew he had been given a second chance and used it to make a positive difference.

Looking back on his journey, he realized that seeking revenge had led him down a dark and dangerous path. But he also knew that it had taught him a valuable lesson about the power of forgiveness and the importance of seeking the truth.

He vowed never to forget that lesson and strive to be better for himself and the people around him. And with that in mind, he set out to make a difference in the world, one small act of kindness at a time.

The Redemption Arc

Once upon a time, a man named Jack had everything going for him. He was a successful businessman with a loving wife and a beautiful daughter. However, one day, his life took a sharp turn for the worse when he discovered that his business partner, Tom, had been embezzling funds from the company. Jack was outraged and felt betrayed, especially because Tom had been his friend for years.

Jack was consumed with anger and decided to seek revenge. He began plotting ways to ruin Tom's life and make him pay for his actions. Jack relentlessly pursued vengeance, and his efforts soon took a toll on his life. He became distant from his family, and his business began to suffer as he spent all his time and energy trying to destroy Tom.

One day, Jack received a call from Tom's lawyer, who asked to meet him in person. Jack was suspicious but decided to go along. When he arrived, he was shocked to discover that Tom had been diagnosed with a terminal illness and had only a few months to live. Tom's lawyer explained that Tom had been trying to make amends for his mistakes by secretly transferring money back into the company's account. He wanted Jack to take over the company after he was gone.

Jack was stunned. All this time, he had been consumed with hate for Tom, not realizing that Tom had been trying to make things right. Jack was resentful and realized he had made a terrible mistake by seeking revenge. He had let his anger consume him, and in doing so, he hurt himself and the people he loved.

Jack visited Tom in the hospital, and the two men had a heart-to-heart conversation. Tom apologized for what he had done, and Jack apologized for his actions. They forgave each other, and Jack finally saw that forgiveness and humility were more powerful than revenge.

Tom's health deteriorated as the months passed, and he eventually died. True to his word, Jack took over the company and worked tirelessly to make it a success. He used the lessons he had learned from his experience with Tom to become a better businessman and person.

In the end, Jack redeemed himself through forgiveness and humility. He realized that revenge was a destructive force that only led to more pain and suffering and that the true path to happiness and success was through kindness and understanding.

With his newfound perspective, Jack reconnected with his family and friends, and they were amazed at the change they saw in him. He was no longer the bitter, angry man he had been before. Instead, he was kind, generous, and empathetic.

Jack always acted with integrity and honesty as he worked to rebuild the company. He was transparent with his employees and clients and earned their trust and respect.

Over time, the company thrived, and Jack became a respected figure in the business world. He was invited to speak at conferences and events, and people looked up to him as a role model.

However, despite all his success, Jack never forgot the lessons he had learned from Tom. He always approached problems with an open mind and a willingness to forgive. He also made a point to help others struggling with the same issues he had faced, offering advice and support whenever possible.

In the end, Jack realized that the redemption arc he had experienced had been a transformative experience. It forced him to confront his flaws and shortcomings and taught him the value of forgiveness and humility. He knew that he had made mistakes and had grown from them.

Returning to his journey, Jack realized he had been given a second chance. He had been allowed to make amends for his past actions and to become the person he had always wanted to be. And he was grateful for every moment of it.

Jack's journey had been a difficult one, but it had also been a rewarding one. He had learned that revenge was a hollow victory and that forgiveness was the only true path to healing.

With this newfound wisdom, Jack lived a fulfilling and meaningful life. He continued to run the company with integrity and was known for his compassion and generosity toward others. He also spent plenty of time with his family and friends, cherishing every moment with them.

Over time, Jack's reputation as a kind and honest business leader grew, and he became a respected figure in the business world and his community.

As he approached the end of his life, Jack felt at peace with himself and the world. He knew that he had made mistakes in the past, but he had done everything in his power to make up for them. He had learned that redemption was possible and that forgiveness was a powerful force that could heal even the deepest wounds.

In the end, Jack's story was one of hope and redemption. It was a reminder that no matter how far we stray from the path, we always have the power to turn things around and make amends for our mistakes. And it was a reminder that forgiveness and humility are the keys to a happy and fulfilling life.

As Jack took his final breaths, surrounded by his loved ones, he knew his legacy would live on. He had shown others that no matter how much they struggled or how many mistakes they made, they always had the power to change and grow.

And with that final thought, Jack closed his eyes, at peace with the knowledge that he had done everything he could to improve the world. His redemption arc had come full circle, and he had become a better person.

The Decay

Detective Ryan had been working on the case for months. He had been searching for the man responsible for the murder of his partner, Detective Smith. His only lead was a witness who had seen a man fleeing the crime scene.

His thirst for revenge had driven Ryan, and he was determined to track down the killer no matter what. He had been going through all the evidence and thought he had finally found a clue. He had found a set of fingerprints on the gun used to kill Smith, and they didn't match any of the suspects on his list.

Ryan's heart raced as he pulled out his phone to call in the evidence. He was so focused on the moment that he didn't hear the door to his apartment opening. Suddenly, he felt a gun pressing into the back of his head.

"Don't move," a voice hissed in his ear. "You're going to come with me."

Ryan's heart sank as he realized he had been caught off guard. He had been so focused on his search for revenge that he hadn't considered that the killer might be closer than he thought.

Ryan tried to stay calm as he was led out of his apartment. He knew his only hope was to stall for time and find a way to escape. But as he was led deeper into the city's darkened alleys, he felt a growing dread.

Finally, they arrived at a dingy warehouse on the outskirts of town. Ryan was pushed inside, and the door was locked behind him. He was alone in the dark and knew he was in serious trouble.

Ryan tried to piece together what had happened while waiting in the dark. How had the killer managed to sneak up on him? And who was behind the decoy that had led him astray for so long?

Finally, a light flickered on, and Ryan found himself face to face with a man he had never seen before. The man was tall, with a gaunt face and piercing blue eyes.

"I've been waiting for you," the man said, his voice low and menacing.

Ryan felt a chill run down his spine as he realized he was face-to-face with the killer. He had been so focused on revenge that he had missed the signs right before him.

"You killed my partner," Ryan said, trying to keep his voice steady. "Why?"

The man smiled coldly. "Your partner was getting too close. He was going to find out the truth."

"What truth?" Ryan asked.

The man stepped closer, and Ryan felt his heart pounding. "The truth about the corruption that runs through this city," the man said. "The truth that no one is willing to face."

Ryan felt fear wash over him as he realized he was over his head. He had been so focused on revenge that he hadn't realized how deep the corruption went.

As the man stepped closer, Ryan knew his only hope was to fight back. He lunged forward, hoping to knock the gun out of the man's hand. But the man was too quick, and Ryan felt a searing pain in his side as the gun went off.

As he fell to the ground, Ryan knew that he had been wrong. Revenge was a hollow victory that led him down a dangerous path. But as he took his final breaths, he knew he had learned a valuable lesson. The actual perpetrators had been hiding in plain sight all along, and it was up to people like him to uncover the truth and bring justice to those who had been wronged.

Ryan lay on the ground, his vision fading as the killer loomed over him. He knew he had only moments to act before it was too late.

Gritting his teeth, he summoned all his strength and launched himself at the man. His hand connected with the gun, knocking it out of the killer's grasp.

They struggled on the ground, each trying to gain the upper hand. Ryan could feel the man's breath on his face as they grappled, and he knew that he was fighting for his life.

Finally, Ryan managed to gain the upper hand and pinned the man to the ground. He saw fear in the killer's eyes as he realized his terror reign was over.

"I won't let you get away with this," Ryan growled, his voice rough with pain and anger.

The killer's eyes narrowed. "You don't understand," he said. "There are others like me. You'll never be able to stop us."

But Ryan didn't listen. He knew he had to bring this man to justice, no matter the cost.

As he held the killer down, Ryan could feel his strength fading. He knew he had been lucky to survive this long, but he couldn't keep going like this forever.

Finally, he heard the sound of approaching sirens and knew his backup had arrived. With one last surge of energy, he hauled the killer to his feet and began to drag him towards the waiting police cars.

It wasn't until they were halfway to the station that Ryan realized how close he had come to losing everything. He had been so focused on revenge that he had nearly lost his life.

But as he looked out the window at the passing cityscape, he knew he had learned a valuable lesson. The corruption in this city ran more profound than he had ever imagined, and it was up to people like him to keep fighting, no matter the cost.

With that thought in mind, Ryan leaned back in his seat, his eyes closed and his hand on his wound. He knew he had a long road ahead of him, but he was ready to face it head-on, no matter the cost.

The sun began to set over the city, casting a warm glow over everything in its path. As Ryan leaned back in his seat, his eyes closed, he could feel a sense of peace wash over him.

He knew that he had accomplished something important today, something that would make a difference in the lives of countless people. And for the first time in a long time, he felt genuinely content.

As the police car wound its way through the city streets, Ryan couldn't help but marvel at the beauty of the world around him. The city was a riot of colors and sounds, each building and street corner teeming with life and energy.

He momentarily let himself get lost in the city's rhythm, allowing the sights and sounds to wash over him like a wave. And as he did, he felt a sense of gratitude for the world and everything in it.

Finally, the car pulled up to the station, and Ryan climbed out, still feeling that sense of peace and contentment. He knew that there was still work to be done, still battles to be fought, but for now, he was happy to bask in the beauty of the world around him.

As he went inside, Ryan couldn't help but think about the unexpected twist that had brought him here. He had been so sure he had the right suspect, convinced he was on the right path.

But in the end, it had been a decoy all along. The true killer had been hiding in plain sight, waiting for the right moment to strike.

It was a humbling realization that only made Ryan more determined to fight. He knew he couldn't let this setback get the best of him and had to keep pushing forward no matter what.

With that thought in mind, Ryan headed to his desk, ready to start the next chapter of his journey. He knew it would be a long and challenging road, but he was prepared to face it head-on, no matter the cost.

As Ryan settled into his chair, he took a moment to reflect on everything that had brought him to this point. The long hours, the sleepless nights, the endless pursuit of justice... it had all been worth it.

He knew there would be more challenges ahead and battles to fight, but he was ready for whatever came his way. He had learned that sometimes, the path to justice was winding, full of twists and turns that he couldn't have predicted.

But he also knew that no matter what, he couldn't give up. He had to keep pushing forward and fighting for what was right, no matter the cost.

As he sat there, surrounded by the bustling energy of the station, Ryan couldn't help but feel a sense of pride in what he had accomplished. He had sought revenge, but in the end, he had found something even more valuable: redemption.

For Ryan, the journey was far from over. But he was ready for whatever lay ahead, armed with the knowledge that he had the strength and the courage to see it through.

As he leaned back in his chair and closed his eyes, Ryan knew that he had found something extraordinary: a sense of purpose and a commitment to justice that would carry him forward, no matter where his path led him next.

And with that, Ryan opened his eyes, feeling a renewed energy and purpose coursing through his veins. He stood up, ready to face the world, and headed out of the station into the city's bright lights and bustling energy.

As he walked, he couldn't help but smile, feeling the warmth of the sun on his face and the energy of the city surrounding him. He knew the road ahead would be long and complex, but he was ready.

The journey had been one of pain, struggle, redemption, and beauty for Ryan. And as he looked at the world around him, he knew there was still so much more to discover and to fight for.

But for now, he was content just to be alive, to feel the sun on his face and the energy of the city surrounding him. And as he walked, he found something extraordinary: the knowledge that he was on the right path, fighting for what was right, no matter the cost.

The Double-Cross

Rachel had been working towards this moment for months. She had put in long hours and nights and sacrificed so much to get this far. She had one goal in mind: revenge.

It all started when her family was killed in a hit-and-run accident. She knew who was responsible, but the legal system failed her. The perpetrator walked free, and Rachel was left with nothing but anger and a burning desire for revenge.

She spent months tracking down the man responsible, doing whatever it took to get close to him. She planned meticulously, learning everything she could about him, his habits, his routines. She even went to work her way into his inner circle, gaining his trust and respect.

Finally, the day of reckoning arrived. Rachel had everything in place, and she was ready to strike. She moved, confronting the man and demanding that he pay for what he had done.

But to her surprise, he didn't fight back. Instead, he calmly told her he had been waiting for this moment and was willing to make amends.

Rachel was stunned. She had expected a fight, a struggle. But instead, the man she had been seeking revenge on was willing to work with her.

Over the next few weeks, Rachel and the man worked together to take down a greater evil: a powerful criminal organization operating in the shadows for years. It was dangerous work, and Rachel was constantly on edge, but she felt a sense of purpose she hadn't felt since her family was alive.

As they worked together, Rachel realized that the man she had sought revenge on wasn't the monster she had made him out to be. He was a flawed human being, just like her, trying to make amends for his mistakes.

The day they finally brought down the criminal organization, Rachel couldn't believe it. It was the end of a long, painful journey, and she felt a sense of relief wash over her.

But there was one final surprise in store for her. As she and the man were celebrating their victory, he revealed that he had been working with the authorities the entire time and that he had been using her to get close to the criminal organization and take them down.

Rachel was shocked, but she also felt a sense of gratitude. She had never imagined that the man she had been seeking revenge on would be her ally, her partner in the fight for justice.

As she walked away from the man, Rachel knew she had found something beautiful: a sense of purpose, a desire for justice, and a newfound respect for forgiveness. And she knew that she would carry those things with her for the rest of her life.

Rachel's emotions were running high as she walked away from the man. She felt betrayed and used, but at the same time, she knew that they had accomplished something great together.

She couldn't help but think about how different things could have been if she had gone through with her original plan of seeking revenge on him. They would have worked against each other, and the criminal organization may have never been brought down.

Despite the surprise ending, Rachel was grateful for the man's help and knew she could never have done it without him. She also realized that she had found something more valuable than revenge- a sense of purpose and the desire to fight for justice.

As she left the man behind, Rachel couldn't help but feel a mix of emotions- the weight of her past lifted off her shoulders, a sense of accomplishment, and a newfound hope for the future.

But her newfound sense of peace was not to last. Just as she reached her car, a group of men jumped her. They were members of the same criminal organization she had helped to bring down.

In a moment of panic, Rachel fought back with all her might. The struggle was intense, and it seemed like she would never get out alive.

Just when she thought it was all over, the man she had sought revenge on appeared out of nowhere, fighting alongside her. They fought together, taking down the men individually until they were the only ones standing.

As they caught their breath, Rachel looked at the man with new eyes. She saw a hero, someone who had been working tirelessly to make amends for his mistakes, even risking his own life in the process.

At that moment, Rachel realized that her revenge had been misplaced. She had been so focused on her pain that she hadn't seen the bigger picture. She had been blind to the fact that the man she sought revenge was trying to make things right.

As they parted ways, Rachel felt a sense of gratitude towards the man, but also towards herself. She had grown, learned the value of forgiveness, and realized that there was a bigger picture than her pain.

She got into her car, started the engine, and drove off into the sunset. She didn't know what the future held, but she knew that she was ready to face it with a renewed sense of purpose and a newfound respect for the power of forgiveness.

As Rachel drove away, she couldn't help but feel a sense of calm wash over her. For the first time in a long time, she felt like she had a clear path ahead. She was ready to move on from the past and embrace the future.

But just as she was about to reach her destination, she received a call. It was the man she had worked with to take down the criminal organization.

"Rachel, we need your help. Another organization's started up, and they're even worse than the last one. We need someone like you on our side."

At first, Rachel was hesitant. She had just been through so much, and getting involved in something dangerous again was daunting. She remembered the sense of purpose and the feeling that she was doing something important.

"Count me in," she said.

The man on the other end of the line smiled. "I knew I could count on you."

And so, Rachel embarked on a new journey that would be even more dangerous and complex than the last. But this time, she was ready. She had learned the value of forgiveness and understood the importance of working together towards a common goal.

As Rachel drove towards her new destination, she couldn't help but feel a sense of excitement. She knew this wouldn't be easy, but she also knew it was something she needed to do. She was ready to fight for justice, and she knew that no matter what happened, she would be able to face it with the strength and resilience that she had gained through her experiences.

With a smile and a sense of purpose, Rachel drove towards her next adventure, ready to take on whatever challenges lay ahead.

As Rachel delved deeper into the new organization, she uncovered a web of secrets and lies. She was shocked to discover that the man she had worked with before was not who he seemed. He had been working with the new organization and only used her as a pawn to take down his enemies.

Rachel was devastated. She couldn't believe that she had been deceived once again. But instead of falling into despair. She had learned from her previous experiences and knew that the only way to take down the new organization was to work with someone she could trust.

She contacted an old acquaintance she had met with the previous organization. This person had always seemed trustworthy, and Rachel hoped she could help her uncover the truth about the new organization.

But as they delved deeper, they realized the organization was even more dangerous than they had thought. They were involved in human trafficking, drug smuggling, and even murder. Rachel and her acquaintance knew they had to act fast to bring them down.

They came up with a plan, one that involved infiltrating the organization from the inside. Rachel would pretend to be a recruit, and her acquaintance would act as her handler. Together, they would gather as much information as possible and bring it to the authorities.

But the plan was not without its risks. Rachel knew she could put herself in danger but knew it was the only way to stop the organization. She uncovered more of their secrets as she went deeper into the organization. She knew the risk was worth it but couldn't help feeling a sense of dread in her stomach.

But as the plan came to fruition, Rachel and her acquaintance gathered enough evidence to bring the organization down. They turned it over to the authorities, and soon, the people responsible were brought to justice.

Rachel was relieved it was finally over, but she couldn't help feeling a sense of emptiness. She had put so much into taking down the organization; now that it was done, she wasn't sure what to do with herself. But as she reflected on her experiences, she had learned so much about herself and what she could do.

With newfound confidence and a renewed sense of purpose, Rachel left the city, ready to start a new chapter. She knew that she would always be prepared to fight for justice and never stop seeking the truth.

As Rachel walked away from the city, she couldn't help but feel a sense of pride in what she had accomplished. She had faced her demons and came out the other side more vital than ever before. But even as she walked away, she knew the work wasn't done.

There were still organizations out there that were doing terrible things. There were still people who needed help and someone to fight for them. And Rachel knew that she was the person to do it.

She knew life would never be easy but was ready for whatever came next. She was no longer the person she had been when she started her journey. She was someone who had faced her fears, who had stood up for what was right, and who had come out the other side more vital than ever before.

And as Rachel looked at the horizon, she knew she was ready for whatever the future had. With a smile and a fire in her heart, she continued walking, prepared for whatever came next.

As Rachel continued her journey, she knew there would be more challenges, more enemies to defeat, and more mysteries to uncover. But she was ready for them all. She had met the most significant challenges of her life and had come out the other side more robust and more determined than ever before.

Rachel had learned that sometimes the people you thought were your enemies were your greatest allies and that the truth was often hidden in the most unexpected places. She had known that revenge was not always the answer and that forgiveness and understanding were powerful tools for change.

As she walked, Rachel looked back at the city she had left behind. It was a city full of pain and suffering but also a city full of hope and promise. She knew there was still work to be done there and that she would one day return to continue the fight.

But for now, Rachel was content to keep walking, exploring, and fighting for what was right. She was a hero, but she was also a human being, and she knew there would be times when she would stumble, fall, and need help.

But Rachel was not afraid. She had faced her fears and knew that no matter what lay ahead, she would always have the strength and courage to meet them. She was a fighter, a survivor, and a hero.

And as Rachel walked on into the sunset, she knew she was not alone. She had friends, allies, and people who believed in her. She had love, hope, and a sense of purpose to guide her on her journey, no matter where it took her.

And so, Rachel continued, ready for whatever came next, knowing that no matter what, she would always be a hero, a champion, and a force for good in the world.

The Twist of Fate

Lucas had always been a happy-go-lucky guy, always ready for a good time and never one to hold a grudge. But everything changed when he discovered his wife had been cheating on him. Suddenly, the laughter was gone, replaced by a seething anger that consumed him completely.

Lucas had never been one for revenge, but this was different. It was personal. He wanted to hurt her the way she had hurt him, to make her suffer and pay for what she had done. And so, he began to plan his revenge.

It wasn't long before he found himself standing outside her lover's apartment, his heart pounding as he prepared to carry out his plan. But just as he was about to knock on the door, he heard a strange noise coming from inside. It sounded like someone was struggling like someone was in pain.

Lucas hesitated momentarily, wondering if he should turn around and walk away. But his anger got the best of him, and he burst through the door, ready to take down his wife's lover.

But what he found inside was not what he was expecting. The man was lying on the ground, his face twisted in agony, clutching his chest. Lucas rushed to his side, feeling a strange sense of déjà vu wash over him.

He remembered the day his father died of a heart attack, the pain and the fear he had felt as he watched his father struggle for breath. And suddenly, it all made sense. The man lying before him was not his wife's lover but a victim of circumstance, a man whose twist of fate had struck down that neither he nor Lucas could have foreseen.

Lucas felt a sense of shame wash over him as he realized what he had almost done. He had been consumed by his anger by his need for revenge and nearly destroyed an innocent man's life. He looked up at the man, who was now unconscious, and felt a surge of guilt wash over him.

Lucas considered walking away momentarily, leaving the man to his fate. But he knew he couldn't do that. And so, he called 911 and waited, watching as the paramedics rushed in and began to work on the man.

As they wheeled the man out of the apartment, Lucas couldn't help but feel a sense of relief. He had almost destroyed an innocent man's life but managed to stop himself just in time. And as he walked out of the apartment, he knew he would never seek revenge again.

Lucas had learned that sometimes, things happen that are out of our control and that there are no villains, only victims of circumstance. He had known that revenge was not the answer and that forgiveness and understanding were the only way to heal the wounds of the past.

As he walked out into the world, ready to start a new chapter, Lucas knew he had been given a second chance to start fresh, leave the past behind, and live a life full of love, hope, and purpose.

Feeling conflicted, Sarah returns to her hotel room and reflects on the day's events. She realizes that the twist of fate that caused the tragedy was no one's fault and that her desire for revenge was misplaced. She also realizes that the person she was seeking revenge was a victim of circumstance, just like the innocent people who were hurt in the accident.

Overwhelmed with emotions, Sarah confronts the person she is seeking revenge on. She goes to their hotel room and knocks on the door. After a few moments, the door opens, and Sarah is face to face with the person she's been seeking revenge on. The person looks at her with a mixture of confusion and fear.

"Please, let me explain," Sarah says, her voice trembling with emotion. "I was wrong to seek revenge on you. I realize now that it was all just a twist of fate neither of us could have foreseen."

The person looks at her, unsure what to make of the situation. "I don't understand," they say.

Sarah takes a deep breath and begins to explain. She tells the person about her brother's accident and how it fueled her desire for revenge.

She explains that she now realizes that a twist of fate caused the accident and that the person she sought revenge was not responsible for what happened.

The person listens to Sarah's story with growing understanding. They are moved by her words and willingness to confront them and admit that she was wrong. They begin to see Sarah in a different light and realize that she's not just seeking revenge but is a kind and compassionate person.

Throughout their conversation, Sarah and the person she was seeking revenge on come to a new understanding of each other. They both realize they have a lot in common and want the same things: to be loved and do good in the world.

As the conversation ends, Sarah and the person she sought revenge on embrace each other, tears streaming down their faces. At that moment, they both feel a sense of connection and understanding that they never thought was possible. They both realize that sometimes, even the worst situations can lead to something beautiful if only we are willing to let go of our desire for revenge and open ourselves up to forgiveness and love.

Days pass, and Sarah returns home from her trip feeling changed. She has a new perspective on life and feels grateful for her experience in Paris. She knows she'll never forget the people and the lessons she learned about forgiveness and letting go of anger.

One day, Sarah receives a phone call from the person she is seeking revenge. They tell her they've been thinking about their conversation in Paris and have come to a new understanding of themselves and their role in the world.

"I want to thank you for showing me that there is another way to live," the person says. "I was so lost before, but now I feel like I have a new purpose in life."

Sarah listens to the person's words with a sense of awe. She realizes that her desire for revenge has inadvertently helped someone find their path in life. She feels a sense of gratitude and humility, knowing that even the most difficult experiences can have unexpected consequences.

Over the years, Sarah stays in touch with the person she seeks revenge, and they become close friends. They both know that their paths in life will never be easy, but they also know that they have each other to lean on.

In the end, Sarah realizes that the twist of fate that brought her to Paris and led her on a path of revenge was a blessing in disguise. It taught her that even in the most challenging situations, there is always a possibility for growth and change. And it showed her that forgiveness and understanding are the keys to a more fulfilling and joyful life.

Years go by, and Sarah never forgets the lessons she learned in Paris. She carries them with her through every triumph and every setback. She knows that life is unpredictable and that sometimes, the people we think are our enemies can be our greatest allies.

Sarah's journey taught her that seeking revenge can only lead to a cycle of anger and pain. Only when we learn to forgive and let go of our anger can we truly move on and find happiness. And although her journey was difficult and painful, she's grateful for every moment because it taught her what it truly means to be alive.

As Sarah looks back on her life, she knows she's changed in ways she never imagined. She's learned to be more patient and understanding, see the world from different perspectives, and appreciate life's beauty in all its complexity.

Although the twist of fate that led her on this journey was painful and complex, it was also a gift. It taught her that life is unpredictable and that we never know what's around the corner. But as long as we stay true to our values and a sense of purpose, we can weather any storm.

As the sun sets on another day, Sarah takes a deep breath and smiles. She knows more challenges will be ahead but is ready for them. She's learned that every challenge is an opportunity to grow, learn, and become a better version of ourselves. And she's grateful for every step of the journey that brought her here.

In the end, Sarah's journey taught her that sometimes, the greatest gift is the unexpected twist of fate. And no matter how dark the road may seem, there's always a light at the end of the tunnel. We must keep moving forward, one step at a time. And with a heart full of love and forgiveness, anything is possible.

The Moral Dilemma

Sophie's heart was heavy with anger and betrayal as she stormed out of the courtroom, the judge's words ringing in her ears. The man who had wronged her so profoundly walked free, acquitted of all charges. The thought of his smug face made her blood boil, and she felt a burning desire for revenge.

She spent months plotting and scheming, gathering evidence, and preparing for the perfect moment to strike. She spent countless sleepless nights obsessing over her plan, her rage growing stronger each day.

But as she stood in the shadows of his house, her hand clenched tightly around the knife she had brought, she suddenly froze. A new realization hit her like a ton of bricks. What if the man she had been seeking revenge on wasn't the real villain in this story? What if he was just a pawn in a greater injustice?

Sophie's mind raced as she thought back to the trial, to the evidence that had been presented. She remembered the defense's argument, claiming that a powerful corporation had coerced their client to take the fall for their misdeeds. She had dismissed it then, too blinded by her pain to see the bigger picture.

But now, as she stood in the darkness, her eyes locked on her target's front door, she couldn't shake the feeling that something wasn't right. What if she was about to commit an act of revenge that would ultimately do more harm than good?

Sophie's hand trembled as she lowered the knife, her mind racing with conflicting thoughts and emotions. She knew she had a choice to make, one that would have far-reaching consequences. She could continue toward revenge, blinded by her anger and pain. Or she could take a step back, look at the bigger picture, and make a choice that would serve the greater good.

It was a difficult decision, one that took her months to make. But in the end, Sophie chooses to put her desire for revenge aside and focus on the greater good. She turned to activism, to fighting for the rights of those wronged by the same corporation that had caused her so much pain. It wasn't an easy road, but it was one that she knew was right.

As time passed, Sophie found peace and purpose in her new path. She still thought about the man who had wronged her, but sadness and empathy replaced her anger. She realized that he, too, had been a victim of the same injustice and that seeking revenge on him would have only perpetuated the cycle of harm.

In the end, Sophie's journey taught her that revenge is never the answer and that sometimes, the only way to find true justice is to focus on the greater good. It was a difficult lesson, but she knew it would guide her for the rest of her life.

As the days passed, the weight of the moral dilemma began to take its toll on the character. They couldn't shake the feeling that seeking revenge was not the right course of action, but their desire for justice still burned fiercely.

One night, while lost in thought, the character was approached by a shadowy figure. The figure revealed that they had been watching the character's actions and knew about the personal nature they had been seeking revenge on.

"The person you're after is not the true villain," the figure said. "They're a victim, just like you were. The real culprit is much bigger and much more dangerous."

The figure explained that a powerful and corrupt group was responsible for the injustices done to the character and the person they had sought revenge on. The group had been operating secretly for years and getting away with their crimes due to their immense power and influence.

The character was torn. On the one hand, it knew that seeking revenge would only perpetuate the cycle of violence and do little to bring true justice. On the other hand, it couldn't simply ignore the wrongs done to them and others.

After much soul-searching, the characters realized they couldn't do it alone. They would need to find allies and work together to bring down the corrupt group and bring true justice. The character set aside their desire for revenge and focused on the greater good.

They reached out to others the corrupt group had wronged, and together, they began gathering information and planning their next move. It wasn't an easy road, but with each step forward, the characters knew they were one step closer to making a real difference.

As they worked to uncover the truth, the characters realized that their moral dilemma had been a test. It forced them to confront the truth about revenge and justice and make a choice that would ultimately define who they were. Finally, the character has chosen to let go of their desire for revenge and focus on something more substantial – the greater good.

Sophie couldn't believe it. Everything she thought she knew had been turned on its head. She was seeking revenge on the right person, but Her heart was heavy with guilt, and she couldn't help but wonder how many people she had hurt.

The next few days were filled with intense reflection for Sophie. She thought about all the people she had harmed, the people she had hurt. She thought about how she had become so consumed with revenge that she had lost sight of the bigger picture.

As she walked through the empty streets of the city, she came to a realization. She could no longer justify her actions. She could no longer continue down this path. She had to make a choice. She could continue toward revenge and destruction or try to make things right.

Sophie decided to put an end to her quest for revenge. She went to the authorities and confessed everything she had done. She was prepared to accept the consequences of her actions, no matter how severe.

The authorities were shocked by her confession. They had been trying to catch her for years but could never pin anything on her. They were surprised to learn that she had turned herself in.

Sophie's confession sparked a chain reaction. It led to the arrest of several high-ranking officials, including the man she had been seeking revenge on. The man had been a victim of greater injustice, just as Sophie had suspected.

Sophie was hailed as a hero by some, but she couldn't bring herself to accept the title. She knew she had done terrible things and would have to live with the consequences for the rest of her life. But she also knew that she had done the right thing.

As Sophie walked out of the courtroom, she felt a sense of relief. She had finally found peace. She knew her journey was far from over, but she was ready to face whatever came her way.

From that day forward, Sophie dedicated her life to helping others. She volunteered at local shelters, worked with children affected by violence, and even started her nonprofit organization. She knew she could never undo the harm she had caused but could impact the world positively.

The moral dilemma that had once consumed her was now a distant memory. Sophie had made her choice, and it was the right one. She had chosen to put the greater good above her desire for revenge, and in doing so, she had found redemption.

Ethan became increasingly obsessed with seeking revenge against the real culprit in the following weeks. He began to neglect his duties as a police officer, instead spending his time investigating the case independently. His wife and colleagues grew increasingly concerned about his behavior, but Ethan refused to listen to their warnings.

One day, Ethan received a call from a mysterious woman who claimed to have information about the case. She arranged to meet him in a deserted alleyway in the middle of the night. When Ethan arrived, he was surprised to find that the woman was the person he had been seeking revenge against.

She explained that she was a victim of the same greater injustice that had led to the death of Ethan's wife. She had been forced into a life of crime to support her sick mother and used as a pawn by the true mastermind behind the scheme. She begged Ethan to forgive her and join forces to take down the real culprit.

Ethan was torn. He had been consumed by his desire for revenge for so long that he wasn't sure if he could let it go. He knew that they were both victims of a cruel twist of fate.

In the end, Ethan makes the difficult decision to forgive the woman and work with her to take down the true culprit. Together, they launched a full-scale investigation that eventually led to the arrest of the mastermind behind the scheme.

As Ethan watched the man being handcuffed, he felt a sense of closure that he had never thought possible. He realized that revenge was not the answer and that forgiveness and working toward the greater good were the paths to healing.

In the following weeks and months, Ethan began to rebuild his life. He returned to his job as a police officer and worked tirelessly to ensure that justice was served for all victims of crime. He also found peace in knowing that his wife's death had not been in vain and that he had played a part in making the world safer.

The memory of his wife would always be with him, but he knew that he could honor her best by living a life of purpose and compassion. And as he looked out at the city skyline, he felt a sense of hope for the first time in a long time. He knew that no matter what challenges lay ahead, he would face them with courage and determination, knowing that he had the power to make a difference in the world.

As the truth of the situation finally dawns on Emily, she faces a choice that will define the rest of her life. She has been consumed with anger and the desire for revenge for so long, but now she sees the bigger picture. She knows what she has to do.

Emily approaches the DA's office and tells him everything, giving him the evidence to reopen the case and bring the corrupt officers to justice. She also tells him about the true culprit, the man who set everything in motion all those years ago. The DA promises to investigate and prosecute whoever is responsible.

Emily turns to leave, her heart heavy with the weight of what she has done. She knows her actions have hurt people, but she hopes the greater good will be served. As she walks away, she feels a sense of relief and a new clarity she has never felt before.

Days pass, and Emily hears that the corrupt officers have been arrested and charged with their crimes. She also hears that the true culprit, the man who had orchestrated everything, has fled the country and is now a fugitive from justice. While it's not the perfect ending she had hoped for, Emily knows that justice has been served and that she has played a part in making it happen.

In the following weeks and months, Emily focuses on rebuilding her life. She takes classes to become a paralegal, determined to make a difference in the world through legal means. She also volunteers at a community center, working with at-risk youth and helping them to stay on the right path.

Through it all, Emily reflects on her journey and moral dilemma. She realizes that seeking revenge may have satisfied her, but it would have only perpetuated the cycle of violence and corruption. Instead, by doing the right thing, Emily has positively impacted the world and found a purpose. She knows the road ahead will be long and complex, but she faces it with hope and determination, ready to make a difference in any way she can.

The Wrong Assumption

Leah sat alone in her car, her grip tight on the steering wheel, her eyes fixed on the modest house in front of her. She had been watching the place for days, waiting for the perfect moment to confront the person she had come to despise so much.

She couldn't believe what he had done to her, how he manipulated her and used her to get what he wanted. The thought of him made her blood boil, and the only thing keeping her from acting on her anger was the knowledge that revenge was a cold dish.

Finally, she saw him emerge from the house, and her heart began to race with anticipation. She exited her car and walked towards him, her fists clenched tightly by her side.

"Hello, Leah," he said with a wry smile. "To what do I owe this unexpected pleasure?"

"You know damn well why I'm here," she spat at him. "You destroyed my life, and I'm here to make you pay for it."

He looked at her with a mix of confusion and concern. "I don't know what you're talking about, Leah. I haven't done anything to hurt you."

She laughed bitterly. "You expect me to believe that? You lied to me, used me, and left me with nothing. I trusted you, and you betrayed me."

He shook his head. "You're making a mistake, Leah. I never meant to hurt you. I was trying to help you."

She scoffed. "Help me? Do you expect me to believe you were trying to help me by destroying my life? I don't think so."

He looked at her with a pained expression. "Leah, please. I'm not the one you should be angry with. You've made a wrong assumption about me, and I can prove it."

She glared at him, her anger bubbling up inside her. "Prove it? How can you prove something like that?"

He sighed and reached into his pocket, pulling out a small envelope. "This is for you," he said. "It's a letter that explains everything. Please read it before you do something you'll regret."

She hesitated for a moment before snatching the envelope from his hand. She tore it open and began to read the letter, her eyes widening in shock as she read the words on the page.

It wasn't him who had destroyed her life. Someone else had used him as a pawn in their twisted game. He had only been trying to protect her, to keep her from harm's way.

Leah felt guilt wash over her as she realized her mistake. She had been so consumed with her anger and pain that she had failed to see the truth.

She looked up at him, tears streaming down her face. "I'm so sorry," she said. "I had no idea."

He smiled sadly at her. "It's okay, Leah. I understand how you feel. But it would help to let go of your anger and focus on the truth. The person responsible for this is still out there, and we need to stop them."

Leah nodded, her mind spinning with the new information. She had been wrong about him all along, and she needed to make it right.

Together, they set out to uncover the truth, to find the person who had caused so much pain and destruction. As they worked side by side, Leah realized that sometimes, the greatest enemy is our assumptions and biases, not the person we seek revenge on.

Rajeev tried to calm himself down and thought about everything he had just learned. He was sure he was right about his revenge plot against Ankit, but now he was questioning everything. He didn't know what to believe anymore.

Ankit noticed Rajeev's confusion and walked over to him. "I know this is a lot to take in, Rajeev. But you need to understand that sometimes things are not what they seem. It's easy to jump to conclusions, but getting all the facts is important before making any decisions."

Rajeev looked up at Ankit, still trying to process everything. "I don't know what to do now. I was so sure that you were the one who had wronged me, but now I don't know what to believe."

Ankit placed a hand on Rajeev's shoulder. "I understand how you're feeling, Rajeev. But I think it's important that you take some time to think about everything. You need to decide if revenge is the answer or if there is a better way to handle the situation."

Rajeev nodded, realizing that Ankit was right. He needed to take some time to think about everything before making any decisions.

As he walked away from Ankit's house, Rajeev couldn't help but feel a sense of relief. He had been carrying so much anger and hatred, and now it felt like a weight had been lifted off his shoulders.

Over the next few days, Rajeev took some time to think about everything he had learned. He realized he had been so focused on revenge that he had lost sight of the bigger picture. He needed to consider what was best for everyone involved, not just himself.

In the end, Rajeev decided to let go of his anger and seek forgiveness from Ankit. He knew that it wouldn't be easy, but he also knew that it was the right thing to do.

When he met with Ankit again, Rajeev apologized for his behavior and explained that he had misunderstood the situation. Ankit was surprised but grateful that Rajeev was willing to put the past behind them and move forward.

As they shook hands and said their goodbyes, Rajeev couldn't help but feel a sense of peace. He had learned an important lesson about forgiveness and understanding, and he knew that it was a lesson he would carry with him for the rest of his life.

As she drove home, the weight of her mistake became heavier with each passing mile. She had been so sure of herself, so convinced of her righteousness, that she had been willing to throw away the life of an innocent person without even giving them a chance to defend themselves.

The thought of it made her sick to her stomach. How could she have been so blind? How could she have been so sure of her judgment that she was willing to condemn someone without hearing their side?

As she approached her house, she saw a figure waiting for her on the porch. It was the person she had wronged, the one she had accused of a crime they didn't commit.

She got out of the car, her heart pounding in her chest. The person stood up and walked towards her, their face unreadable.

"I owe you an apology," she said, her voice barely above a whisper. "I was wrong. I made a mistake. I'm so sorry for accusing you of something you didn't do."

The person looked at her for a moment, then slowly nodded. "I forgive you," they said. "But I want you to understand something. I felt accused of a crime because I thought you were doing the right thing. You were so convinced of your moral superiority that you didn't even consider the possibility that you might be wrong."

The weight of their words hit her like a ton of bricks. She had been so sure of herself, convinced that she was the story's hero, and never even stopped considering the possibility that she might be the villain.

"I know," she said, tears streaming down her face. "I was so wrong. I can't even begin to imagine how you must feel right now. But please, let me make it up to you. I'll do whatever it takes to make things right."

The person looked at her for a moment, then nodded. "Okay," they said. "But first, I need you to understand something. I felt accused of a crime because you assumed I had something to gain from it. You thought I was trying to get ahead by sabotaging someone else. But the truth is, I had nothing to do with it. I was just in the wrong place at the wrong time. The real perpetrator was someone else entirely."

The revelation hit her like a ton of bricks. She had been so focused on her assumptions that she had never even considered the possibility that someone else was behind it all.

"I.... I had no idea," she said, her voice barely above a whisper.

"I know," the person said, nodding. "But that's the thing. We can't always trust our assumptions. We must be willing to question them, to see the other side of the story. Otherwise, we'll end up hurting the wrong people."

The words hit her hard; she knew she would never forget them. She had learned a hard lesson, but it was a lesson that she would carry with her for the rest of her life. The importance of questioning assumptions and seeing the other side of the story. And, more importantly, the importance of admitting when she was wrong and making amends for her mistakes.

With the words hanging in the air, the two women sat silently for a moment, each lost in their thoughts.

Finally, Emily spoke. "I had no idea," she said quietly. "I'm so sorry, Sarah. I had no right to accuse you of those things."

Sarah looked at her for a moment before responding. "I understand why you thought what you did," she said. "But I can't tell you how relieved I am that you believe me now. It's been a nightmare trying to clear my name."

The two women sat silently for a moment more before Emily spoke again. "Is there anything I can do to make it up to you?" she asked.

Sarah thought for a moment before responding. "Well," she said slowly, "there is one thing. The person who did what I was accused of was never caught. I've been trying to find out who it was for months, but I've hit a dead end. I don't know if you know anyone who could help me?"

Emily nodded. "I might," she said. "I'll make a few calls and see what I can do."

Emily used her connections over the next few days to dig deeper into the case. It wasn't long before she found the evidence she sought and brought it to Sarah.

"It's not who you thought it was," she said, handing Sarah a file. "The real culprit was someone we never suspected."

Sarah took the file, her hands shaking slightly. As she read through it, her eyes widened in disbelief. "I can't believe it," she whispered. "I had no idea."

Emily put a hand on her shoulder. "I'm sorry it took so long to find out," she said. "But I'm glad we finally got to the truth."

She knew she still had a long road ahead to clear her name completely, but she was on the right track for the first time in months. And as she looked up at the blue sky above her, she felt a glimmer of hope that maybe, just maybe, things would finally be okay.

After the shock of the truth, Maria felt a wave of sadness. She had spent months plotting her revenge, consumed with anger and hatred, only to realize it was all based on a false assumption.

Maria was now faced with the harsh reality that she had been wrong all along. She had wronged someone who had only been trying to help her, and she had let her own emotions cloud her judgment.

As she stood there in silence, tears streaming down her face, she realized she had lost something valuable. She had lost her sense of self-respect and her moral compass. She had allowed her desire for revenge to consume her, and in the end, she had become no better than the person she had been seeking revenge against.

Maria turned to Roberto and whispered, "I'm so sorry."

Roberto looked at her with a mixture of pity and sadness. "It's okay, Maria. You didn't know."

"I was wrong," she said, her voice barely above a whisper. "I was so wrong."

Roberto put his arm around her, and they stood silently, watching the sunset over the horizon.

At that moment, Maria knew she had a long road ahead. She would need to make amends for what she had done, and she would need to learn to forgive herself for her mistakes.

But for now, she was content to stand there with Roberto, watching the world go by and slowly healing the wounds of her soul.

After the funeral, Sarah sat alone in her room, feeling the world's weight on her shoulders. She knew she had made a terrible mistake and now had to endure the consequences. As she looked out the window, tears streaming down her face, she realized that revenge had consumed her, and she had lost sight of what mattered.

At that moment, Sarah promised never to let revenge cloud her judgment again. She would honor her father's memory by improving the world, not seeking vengeance for his death.

From that day forward, Sarah dedicated herself to helping others, working tirelessly to impact the world positively. She used the lessons she learned from her father to inspire and guide her, and she never forgot the cost of revenge.

In the end, Sarah found redemption in the kindness and love she showed to others. She knew that her father would be proud of the person she had become and that his memory would live on through the good she did in the world.

The Unexpected Ally

Sophie had been wronged, and she was out for revenge. For years, she sought a way to take down the man who had ruined her life, David. He had caused her family business to go bankrupt, forcing them to sell their home and live in poverty.

Sophie had spent years working on a plan to get revenge. She had been tracking David's movements, monitoring his phone calls and emails, and gathering evidence of his wrongdoing. And finally, she had the perfect opportunity to strike.

Sophie waited until David was alone in his office late at night. She broke in and was ready to confront him, but David spoke before she could do anything.

"I know what you're here for," he said, his voice calm and steady. "But before you do anything, I must tell you something."

David's words took Sophie aback. She had expected him to be defensive, to deny everything. But instead, he seemed almost relieved to see her.

"I know you think I'm the one who ruined your life," David continued. "But that's not entirely true. Yes, I was involved in the business deal that caused your family to go bankrupt. But I was just a small player in a much bigger game."

Sophie was confused. She had always assumed that David was the mastermind behind everything.

"There were others involved, people with much more power and influence than me," David explained. "They wanted to take down your family's business for their gain and used me to do it. I was just a pawn in their game."

Sophie was stunned. She had never considered the possibility that there were other people involved.

"But why are you telling me this now?" she asked.

"Because I want to help you," David said. "I know what it's like to be used and manipulated. And I know that you've been hurt. But you can't take down these people alone. They're too powerful. You need an ally."

Sophie was hesitant. She didn't trust David, but his words made sense.

"What do you suggest we do?" she asked.

David laid out a plan to take down the people who had caused Sophie's family to go bankrupt and ruin her life. It was risky, but it was the only option they had.

Sophie agreed to work with David, but she couldn't shake the feeling that there was something he wasn't telling her.

As they worked together, Sophie began to see a different side of David. He was intelligent, resourceful, and determined to make things right. And he seemed genuinely remorseful for what he had done to her family.

Sophie realized that she had misjudged him. He wasn't the monster she had made him out to be in her mind. He was a human being, just like her, who had made mistakes.

As they continued their mission, they encountered many obstacles and close calls. But they overcame them together, using their unique skills and knowledge.

In the end, they were successful. They took down the people who ruined Sophie's life, and David revealed the ultimate sacrifice he had to make to ensure their plan succeeded.

Sophie was stunned by David's revelation but realized he had been telling the truth. She had misjudged him and, in doing so, had almost lost the chance to make things right.

As they parted ways, Sophie knew that she would never forget the lessons she had learned. Revenge was not always the answer. Sometimes, you need an unexpected ally to help you achieve your goals. And sometimes, you need to look beyond your assumptions to see the truth.

As Lucy pondered her next move, she realized that she had quickly jumped to conclusions about Taylor's intentions. She remembered all the times that Taylor had been there for her, offering advice and support, and she couldn't believe that she had ever doubted their friendship.

Lucy's mind raced as she tried to devise a plan to make amends with Taylor. She knew that she had to make things right but also that it wouldn't be easy.

Just as Lucy was about to give up hope, she received a call from Taylor. "Lucy, I'm sorry for what I did," Taylor said. "I know it wasn't fair to you, and I want to make things right."

Taylor's words took Lucy aback. She had expected Taylor to be angry with her, not apologetic. But as they spoke, Lucy realized that their misunderstanding had just as hurt Taylor as she had been.

Together, Lucy and Taylor worked to repair their friendship. They talked through their miscommunication and worked to build a stronger bond. Ultimately, Lucy was grateful for Taylor's unexpected allyship and the chance to repair their relationship.

As Lucy reflected on her journey, she realized she had learned an essential lesson about assumptions and misunderstandings. She knew that she would never again jump to conclusions without first taking the time to understand the whole picture. As she looked toward the future, she felt hopeful that she could continue to grow and learn from her mistakes.

As the days passed, the characters worked alongside their unexpected ally to defeat their mutual enemy. With each passing day, they grew to trust each other more and more, and the surface began to realize that their initial assumption had been entirely wrong.

The ally shared with the character the true story of their past, and the character came to understand the pain and suffering they had gone through. They had been working in secret to take down the enemy, but their actions had been misconstrued by the character, who had only seen them as an obstacle to their revenge.

As they worked together, the character began to see the ally in a new light. They realized their ally was a good person who had been caught up in a difficult situation, just like they had been. They began to feel remorse for how they treated the ally and vowed to make it up to them in any way they could.

Finally, after weeks of planning and preparation, the character and their ally implemented their plan. They worked together seamlessly, and their enemy was defeated without a hitch. The texture felt a sense of relief, knowing that they had finally accomplished what they had set out to do. But more than that, they felt a sense of gratitude towards their ally, who had been there for them when they needed it the most.

As they parted ways, the character couldn't help but feel a sense of loss. They had come to rely on their ally, and the thought of not having them by their side was difficult to bear. But they knew they would never forget what their ally had done for them and vowed to always be there in return.

Ultimately, the character learned an important lesson about forgiveness and trust. It realized that sometimes, the people they least expect to help them could be their greatest allies. And they knew that they would never again judge someone based on assumptions and hearsay.

Despite his frustration, Ryan couldn't help but appreciate the beauty of the sunset as he stood on the edge of the pier. The sky's oranges, pinks, and purples were so striking that it took his breath away. But his mind was elsewhere, consumed by the thought of revenge.

Just then, he heard footsteps approaching from behind. He turned to see a figure coming. It was the person he had been seeking revenge on.

Ryan's anger flared up again as he stepped forward. "What are you doing here?" he demanded.

The person raised their hands defensively. "I came to talk to you," they said. "I want to explain myself."

Ryan hesitated but then nodded. "Fine. Talk."

And so the person told Ryan their story- how they had been working to help him all along but had been misunderstood. They had been trying to protect him, not harm him.

Ryan's anger slowly dissipated as he listened, and he began to see the situation from a new perspective. The person had been an unexpected ally, and Ryan had misjudged them.

As the sunset faded into darkness, Ryan made a decision. He would let go of his anger and work together with the person to achieve their shared goals. The unexpected ally had changed everything, and Ryan knew their new partnership would be more robust than anything he could have accomplished alone.

John stared at Sam with a mix of disbelief and gratitude. He had been so convinced that Sam was the one who had wronged him that he never thought to look at the situation from a different angle. He felt foolish for letting his anger and hurt cloud his judgment.

Sam watched John's reaction and couldn't help but feel a sense of pride. He had always believed in second chances, and seeing John understand the truth was a victory.

As they returned to the car, John couldn't help but feel a sense of relief wash over him. He had been carrying the weight of his anger and thirst for revenge for far too long, and it felt like a burden had been lifted off his shoulders.

In the car, John turned to Sam and spoke, his voice heavy with emotion.

"I don't know how to thank you, Sam. I would never have been able to move on from this if it weren't for you."

Sam smiled, "No thanks necessary, John. I'm just glad I was able to help you see the truth. We all make mistakes; how we learn and grow from them matters."

John nodded, his eyes misty with tears, "You're right, Sam. I have a lot of learning and growing to do, but I'm ready for it now. Thank you."

As they drove away, John couldn't help but feel a sense of hope for the first time in a long time. He knew that moving on wouldn't be easy, but with Sam's unexpected help, he felt he finally had a chance to start fresh.

The experience taught John a valuable lesson about the dangers of assumptions and the power of forgiveness. He knew he had a lot of work to do, but with a newfound perspective and the help of an unexpected ally, he was ready to take on whatever challenges came.

As the dust settled and the truth was revealed, Sarah and Mark looked at each other with mixed emotions. Sarah felt relief and guilt, realizing she had been wrong about Mark. She had allowed her anger and pain to blind her to the truth and had almost ruined her chance at happiness.

Mark, on the other hand, felt a sense of vindication mixed with sadness. He had spent so much time trying to prove his innocence, and now that the truth was out, he realized just how much he had lost. But simultaneously, he felt relieved that he could finally move on from this nightmare.

As they looked at each other, they realized that a shared tragedy had brought them together. At the same time, they had started as enemies but ended up as unexpected allies. They had both been wronged and sought justice, but in the end, they had found solace in each other.

They stood there for an eternity, looking into each other's eyes. And at that moment, they both knew that they had found something special. Something pure and true.

As they walked away from the courthouse, hand in hand, Sarah and Mark knew that they would face many challenges ahead. But they also knew that they could meet them together. And that was all that mattered.

The Betrayed Assistant

Sarah had been working as an executive assistant for Mr. Thompson for over five years. She had always been loyal, hardworking, and dedicated to her job. But one day, everything changed.

Mr. Thompson had promised Sarah a promotion and a significant pay raise. However, when the time came, he hired someone else for the position and gave Sarah no explanation for his decision. Feeling betrayed and disrespected, Sarah decided to quit.

Sarah spent months looking for a new job but couldn't find anything suitable. In the meantime, Mr. Thompson's company was going through some financial difficulties. Sarah kept a close eye on the company's progress and noticed that the situation was worsening daily. She decided to take matters into her own hands.

Sarah got a job at a competing company and started to work her way up the corporate ladder. She connected with essential people in the industry and learned all she could about Mr. Thompson's business. She discovered that he had made some poor decisions, and his company was on the brink of bankruptcy.

Sarah started to sabotage Mr. Thompson's business secretly. She leaked confidential information to his competitors, did fake online reviews that tarnished the company's reputation, and ensured their marketing campaigns failed.

Mr. Thompson was clueless about what was happening. He thought his company's troubles were due to the economic downturn, and he never suspected that Sarah was behind all of this.

One day, Sarah received a call from Mr. Thompson. He was desperate and asked for her help to save his company. Sarah agreed to meet him in person.

When they met, Mr. Thompson was shocked to see Sarah. He asked her how she had climbed the corporate ladder so quickly. Sarah smiled and said, "You should have given me the promotion I deserved."

Mr. Thompson then pleaded with her to help him save his company. He promised to make things right and give her the promotion she deserved. But Sarah had other plans. She told him that she was going to take over his company.

Mr. Thompson laughed and said, "You're just an assistant. You can't run a company like this."

Sarah replied, "You underestimated me, Mr. Thompson. I learned everything I needed to know about running a business from you. And now, it's time for me to take over."

With that, Sarah handed Mr. Thompson a piece of paper. It was the deed to his company. She had bought it using her connections and her savings.

Mr. Thompson was speechless. He had lost everything, and Sarah had taken everything he had worked for. Sarah had her revenge, which she had done in the most satisfying way possible.

As Sarah walked out of Mr. Thompson's office, she couldn't help but smile. She had proven to herself and Mr. Thompson that she was more than just an assistant. She was a force to be reckoned with and ready to take on anything that came her way.

Sarah walked out of Mr. Thompson's office with her head held high, feeling like she had finally achieved her deserved success. She had spent years working tirelessly for Mr. Thompson, only to be betrayed and left with nothing. But now, she owned a successful company, and Mr. Thompson was left with nothing but regret.

Sarah worked tirelessly over the next few weeks to turn Mr. Thompson's struggling company around. She used her expertise and knowledge of the industry to implement changes that brought in new customers and increased profits. Her hard work and dedication paid off, and the company quickly became a significant player in the industry again.

As news of Sarah's success spread, she started to receive offers from other companies who wanted her to work for them. But Sarah had no interest in leaving her own company. She had put too much work into it, and she was determined to see it succeed.

Mr. Thompson, on the other hand, had fallen into a deep depression. He had lost everything he had worked for and had no idea what to do next. He reached out to Sarah, hoping to make amends and work with her. But Sarah had no interest in working with someone who had betrayed her.

Ultimately, Mr. Thompson was forced to start over from scratch while Sarah continued to build her empire. She had achieved her revenge in the most satisfying way possible by proving that hard work and dedication can pay off and that loyalty should always be rewarded.

Years later, Sarah looked back on her journey with pride. She had come a long way from being a loyal assistant to Mr. Thompson. She had faced setbacks and challenges but never gave up on her dream. And now, she owns a successful company that is making a difference in the world.

As Sarah sat in her office, looking out at the city skyline, she couldn't help but smile. She had achieved her revenge, but more importantly, she had achieved her dreams. She proved that anything is possible with hard work, determination, and some revenge.

Sarah continued to lead her company to success, never forgetting the lessons she had learned as an assistant. She always treated her employees respectfully and kindly, never forgetting how Mr. Thompson treated her. She knew that the key to success was not just hard work but also treating others the way you wanted to be treated.

As her company grew and thrived, Sarah became known as a trailblazer in the industry, inspiring others to follow in her footsteps. She even started a mentorship program for young women, hoping to pass on the lessons she had learned throughout her journey.

In the end, Sarah achieved more than just revenge. She had created something significant that made a difference in people's lives. She had shown that even when faced with adversity, one can rise above it and achieve greatness. And that, in the end, is the greatest revenge of all.

The Jilted Lover

Caroline had always dreamed of her wedding day. She imagined walking down the aisle in a beautiful white gown, surrounded by her friends and family, with her fiancé waiting for her at the altar. But all those dreams came crashing down when she discovered that her fiancé, Mark, had been cheating on her.

Caroline was devastated. She had spent years with Mark, planning their future together. They had talked about having children and growing old together, and now all those plans were gone. Mark had betrayed her, and Caroline was left with a broken heart.

At first, Caroline didn't know what to do. She spent her days crying and trying to understand what had happened. She decided to get revenge on Mark by staging a fake wedding.

Caroline spent months planning the fake wedding. She found a look-alike bride, rented a venue, and even had a custom-made wedding gown designed. She invited Mark's friends, family, and some of her own and waited for the wedding day.

On the day of the wedding, Caroline was nervous. She knew what she was doing was risky but determined to do it. She saw Mark's face in the crowd and felt anger and betrayal.

The fake ceremony was beautiful. Caroline's look-alike bride was stunning, and everyone was swept up in the moment's emotion. But then, at the reception, Caroline revealed the truth.

"Thank you all for coming to my wedding," Caroline said, her voice shaking with emotion. "But I have a confession to make. It is not a real wedding. I staged this whole thing to get revenge on my ex-fiancé, Mark."

The room went silent. Everyone was staring at Caroline, wondering what was going to happen next.

"I wanted to show Mark what it felt like to be betrayed and humiliated in front of everyone he knows," Caroline continued. "But now I realize what he did to me was much worse. He broke my heart, so I will never forgive him."

Caroline turned to Mark, standing at the back of the room, looking ashamed.

"You thought you could get away with cheating on me and calling off our wedding," Caroline said, her voice rising. "But I'm not going to let you get away with it. You are a liar and a cheat, and you don't deserve anyone's love."

The room erupted into applause. Caroline's friends and family came over to hug her, telling her how proud they were of her. Mark slunk out of the room, humiliated and defeated.

Caroline realized at that moment that revenge was not the answer. She had shown Mark what it felt like to be betrayed and humiliated but also hurt herself. She had let her anger and hurt consume her, and now she was left with nothing but a sense of emptiness.

But she also realized that she had the power to move on. She had the power to heal her broken heart and find happiness again. And that was the greatest revenge of all.

Caroline took a deep breath and decided it was time to move on from Mark and the pain he had caused her. She knew it would take time, but she was determined to focus on herself and her happiness.

As the weeks and months went by, Caroline started to feel better. She spent time with her friends, traveled to new places, and tried new hobbies. She realized there was so much more to life than being in a relationship and that she could achieve anything she wanted.

One day, while out with her friends at a local coffee shop, Caroline met a man named Jake. They struck up a conversation and immediately hit it off. Jake was kind, funny, and genuinely interested in getting to know Caroline.

They started dating, and Caroline found that she could open up to Jake in a way she had never been able to with Mark. He listened to her, supported her, and made her feel loved.

Eventually, Jake asked Caroline to marry him, and she said yes. She knew that this time, it was different. She was no longer seeking revenge or trying to prove something to herself or anyone else. She was simply happy.

Caroline and Jake married in a beautiful ceremony surrounded by friends and family. As they exchanged their vows, Caroline felt a sense of peace and contentment wash over her. She knew she had finally found the love and happiness she had been searching for.

Looking back on her fake wedding, Caroline realized it had been a turning point. It had been the moment when she realized that revenge was not the answer and that the only way to move on from the pain of her past was to focus on her happiness.

In the end, Caroline found a love that was real, and that was the greatest revenge of all. Caroline's heart swelled with joy, and she knew she had finally found the happiness she had been searching for. She had gone from being a jilted lover seeking revenge to a woman who had found true love and forgiveness.

As she looked around the room, she saw Mark's stunned expression. It was clear that he had not expected this turn of events. Caroline could see the regret in his eyes, and for the first time, she felt a sense of pity for him. She knew he would never experience the love and happiness she had found with Jake.

Caroline's journey had been long and complex, but it had led her to this moment. She had been hurt and betrayed but refused to let those experiences define her. Instead, she used them as fuel to become her best version.

Caroline knew she had won as she walked down the aisle with her new husband. She had found the love and happiness she deserved and found peace within herself. She had let go of the anger and bitterness that had consumed her for so long and had finally moved on.

Ultimately, Caroline's revenge had been to live a happy and fulfilling life. She had shown Mark that his actions could not break her and that she could rise above them. It was a victory that could never be taken away from her and one that she would cherish for the rest of her days.

The Framed Innocent

John had always been an upstanding citizen. He worked hard, paid his taxes, and was loved by his family and friends. But one fateful day, everything changed.

John was walking home from work when a group of men attacked and robbed him. They took his wallet, watch, and phone, leaving him bleeding on the sidewalk.

When the police arrived, they found John's wallet and phone in the possession of another man, who was promptly arrested. But in a shocking turn of events, the man accused John of being part of the robbery and pointed to a security camera footage that seemingly showed John taking part in the crime.

Despite John's protests of innocence, he was arrested, tried, and convicted of robbery. He was sentenced to 10 years, an unjust punishment for a crime he had not committed.

John struggled to accept his new reality during his first few years of imprisonment. Dangerous criminals surrounded him, and he feared for his life every day. But as time passed, he became determined to prove his innocence and seek justice for the wrongful conviction that had ruined his life.

John began to study law in prison, using every spare moment to learn about the legal system and how he could fight for his freedom. He also contacted a private investigator, who agreed to help him gather evidence to clear his name.

Over the years, John uncovered a web of lies and deceit that had led to his wrongful conviction. He discovered that the man who had accused him of the crime was a notorious gang member who had committed several similar robberies in the area. The gang had used John as a scapegoat, framing him for the crime to avoid suspicion.

With the help of his private investigator, John gathered enough evidence to prove his innocence and expose the real criminals. He presented his case to the court, and after a long and grueling trial, the truth was finally revealed.

The real criminal was arrested and convicted, and John was released from prison, a free man. But his fight for justice was not over yet. He was determined to seek revenge on the person who had framed him and ruined his life.

John tracked down the man responsible and confronted him in a dramatic showdown. He presented the evidence he had gathered, and the man had no choice but to confess to the crime.

In the end, John achieves his revenge. He had cleared his name, regained his freedom, and exposed the corruption and injustice that led to his wrongful conviction. He had shown that justice could prevail even in the face of overwhelming odds. With his name cleared and his freedom restored, John found a new purpose in life. He advocated for criminal justice reform, using his experience to fight for the rights of the wrongfully accused and convicted.

John also reconnected with his family and friends, who had stood by him throughout his ordeal. He was grateful for their unwavering support and vowed never to take their love and loyalty for granted again.

As for the man who had framed him, John felt a sense of closure, knowing he had been brought to justice. He knew that the man would never be able to hurt anyone else again, and that was enough for him.

John's journey had been long and painful, but he had emerged more robust and resilient. He had proven that there was always hope for redemption and justice, even in the darkest times.

Looking back on his experience, John realized he had been given a second chance at life. He had been allowed to start anew, rebuild his reputation, and make a difference in the world. And he was determined to make the most of it.

John knew that he would never forget the injustice that had been done to him, but he also knew that he would not let it define him.

He had proven that he was a survivor and that he had the strength and courage to overcome any obstacle that came his way. In the end, John's story became an inspiration to many. His perseverance and determination in the face of adversity showed that no matter how bleak a situation may seem, there is always a way forward.

John's experience also highlighted the flaws in the criminal justice system and the importance of fighting for justice and fairness for all. He became a beacon of hope for those wrongfully accused or convicted, and his story served as a rallying cry for change.

As John looked out at the world, he felt a sense of pride and accomplishment. He had come a long way from the day he was wrongfully accused and convicted. He had faced his fears, overcome his challenges, and emerged victorious.

And as he looked ahead to the future, John knew there would be new challenges and obstacles to overcome. But he was ready for them. He had proven that he was a fighter, and he was confident that he could overcome anything that came his way.

Finally found the justice he had been seeking, but he had also found something more substantial - his inner strength and resilience. And he knew that with that strength, he could achieve anything he wanted.

The Bullied Teen

High school was supposed to be the best years of his life, but it was a nightmare for David. He was constantly teased and bullied by the popular kids, who seemed to take pleasure in making his life miserable.

David was brilliant but kept his head down and tried to avoid trouble. But one day, he had had enough. He decided to get revenge on the kids who had made his life a living hell.

David was a computer whiz and knew he could use his skills to wreak havoc on the popular kids' lives. He started by hacking into the school's computer system and altering the grades of the popular kids. He knew that their high grades were the key to getting into the colleges of their dreams, and he wanted to take that away from them.

At first, David felt satisfied as he watched the popular kids struggle to understand why their grades had suddenly dropped. But as time passed, he began to feel guilty about what he had done. He knew that he was no better than the bullies who had tormented him.

But it was too late to turn back now. The damage had been done, and the popular kids were feeling the consequences of their actions. They had been denied admission to their preferred colleges and were forced to face the reality that their behavior had real-world consequences.

As news of the grade hacking spread, the popular kids were humiliated and ostracized by their peers. They had lost the respect of the school community, and they knew they had only themselves to blame.

David watched from the sidelines, torn between his feelings of satisfaction and his guilt. He knew what he had done was wrong, but he also knew that the popular kids had brought this upon themselves.

In the end, David realized that revenge was not the answer. He knew that he had to find a way to forgive the popular kids and move on with his life. He started to focus on his studies and his passion for computer science, using his skills for good instead of for revenge.

Years later, David looked back on his high school years with a sense of clarity. He realized that the bullying he had endured had taught him a valuable lesson - the importance of empathy and kindness. And he knew that he had the power to make a difference in the world, one computer program at a time.

As he pursued his passion for computer science, David became known for his innovative projects and dedication to using technology for the greater good. He had learned from his mistakes and knew his skills could be used to help others.

David also started mentoring other students interested in computer science, sharing his knowledge and skills with those who needed it most. He wanted to give back to the community that had supported him during his darkest days, and he knew that his expertise could help others achieve their goals.

As David continued to thrive in his field, he realized that his experience with bullying had given him a unique perspective on life. He had learned that revenge was not the answer and that kindness and empathy were the keys to a happy and fulfilling life.

David was no longer the bullied teen he had once been. He had grown into a confident and booming adult with a deep sense of purpose and a commitment to making the world a better place.

Looking back on his high school years, David knew he had been through a difficult time. But he also knew that he had emerged from that experience more robust and resilient than ever. And he knew he could achieve anything he set his mind to with his skills and passion.

Despite his hardships, David learned valuable lessons he would carry with him for the rest of his life. He understood the importance of standing up for himself and others, using his skills for good, and always maintaining a positive attitude.

As he moved forward, David remained committed to his passion for technology and innovation. He continued to develop new projects and explore new avenues of research, always striving to impact the world positively.

But more than that, David remained committed to the idea that kindness and empathy were the keys to a fulfilling life. He believed that by treating others with respect and compassion, he could help create a better world for everyone.

Ultimately, David's experience with bullying taught him some of life's most important lessons. He had learned to overcome adversity, stand up for what was right, and never give up on his dreams. And he knew that, with these lessons in his heart, he could achieve anything he set his mind to.

David continued to live with passion and purpose, striving to impact the world positively. His experience with bullying shaped him into the kind, empathetic, and determined person he is today.

He remained dedicated to helping others and became an advocate for those who had experienced bullying or other forms of mistreatment. He used his time and resources to support organizations that prevented bullying and promoted kindness and respect.

As the years passed, David's reputation as a talented innovator and a kind-hearted individual continued to grow. Many admired and respected him, and his work inspired countless others to pursue their passions and make a positive difference in the world.

In the end, David knew that his experience with bullying had been a difficult and painful chapter in his life. But he also knew it had given him the strength, resilience, and empathy he needed to succeed. And he was grateful for every lesson he had learned along the way.

The Greedy Business Partner

John and Mark had been friends since college and always dreamed of starting a business together. After years of planning and hard work, they finally launched their own tech company, quickly becoming a huge success. They were both thrilled to live their dream and make a difference.

However, John began to change as the company grew more extensive and profitable. He became increasingly greedy and power-hungry, manipulating the finances to his advantage. He began embezzling money from the company, transferring funds into secret accounts that only he had access to.

At first, Mark had no idea what was happening. However, as he began to notice discrepancies in the financial statements, he became suspicious. He hired an accountant to investigate, and it wasn't long before the truth was revealed. John had been stealing from the company for years, siphoning off millions of dollars for his gain.

Mark was devastated. He had put his heart and soul into the company and couldn't believe that John had betrayed him in this way. But he was determined to make things right. He knew he had to get revenge.

Mark's first move was to confront John directly. He confronted him about the embezzlement and demanded that he return the money. But John was unapologetic. He told Mark that he deserved the money and had no intention of returning it.

That's when Mark came up with a plan. He knew he couldn't beat John in a physical or legal battle, but he realized he had something even more powerful: access to John's financial information.

Mark used his skills in computer hacking to gain access to John's bank accounts, investment portfolios, and other financial records. He started slowly draining John's accounts, siphoning off small amounts of money at a time to avoid suspicion.

At first, John didn't even notice. But as the months passed and his accounts dwindled, he became increasingly panicked. He had no idea what was happening or how to stop it.

Meanwhile, Mark was enjoying his revenge. He felt a sense of satisfaction every time he transferred money out of John's accounts, knowing that he was taking away the very thing that had driven John to betray him in the first place.

It wasn't long before John's finances were completely drained. He has left with a mountain of debt and a shattered reputation. He had lost everything he had worked so hard for and had no one to blame but himself.

Mark, on the other hand, was thriving. He had taken over the company and grown it even more significantly. He had proven that honesty and integrity were the keys to success, and he had exacted his revenge on the man who had tried to bring him down.

In the end, John was left to pick up the pieces of his life while Mark continued to build a legacy of innovation and integrity. It was a harsh lesson but one that both men would never forget.

Alex couldn't believe what he was hearing. He had trusted his partner for years and was now accused of stealing from their company. His mind was racing with questions, but he couldn't find the words to ask them.

"I have evidence, Alex. Bank statements, receipts, everything. You've been taking money from the company for months," Jack said, his voice brutal and unforgiving.

Alex felt his stomach drop. He had been so careful, so sure that he could cover his tracks. But now, it was all crashing down around him.

"What do you want?" Alex asked, his voice barely above a whisper.

"I want you to resign. Please hand over everything you've taken, and I want you out of my life. If you don't comply, I'll go to the authorities and have you arrested," Jack said, his tone leaving no room for negotiation.

Alex nodded slowly, defeated. He knew he had no choice but to do as Jack asked. As he packed up his things and left the office, he couldn't help but feel a burning sense of anger and resentment towards his former partner.

He spent the next few weeks in a daze, trying to figure out what he would do next. He knew he couldn't just let Jack get away with ruining his life.

It was then that Alex hatched a plan. He used his computer skills to track Jack's bank accounts and investments, slowly siphoning off money from each one. At first, he was cautious, only taking small amounts to avoid detection. But as time passed, his confidence grew, and he began taking larger and larger sums.

It wasn't long before Jack started to notice that something was wrong. Money was disappearing from his accounts, and he couldn't figure out where it was going. He hired a team of investigators to track down the theft's source, but they came up empty-handed.

Meanwhile, Alex was living high, using the stolen money to buy fancy cars, expensive clothes, and exotic vacations. He was careful to keep his spending under the radar, never flaunting his wealth in front. But eventually, Jack's investigators caught a break. They traced the stolen money back to Alex, who was arrested and charged with embezzlement.

Alex was sentenced to several years in prison but didn't care. He finally got his revenge on Jack, which was all that mattered. Sitting in his cell, he couldn't help but smile at the thought of his former partner, bankrupt and ruined just like he had been.

However, as time passed, Alex began to realize the actual cost of his revenge. He had lost everything - his job, reputation, and freedom. He regretted his actions and knew he had let his anger and greed get the best of him.

While in prison, Alex began reflecting on his choices and life. He realized he had made a mistake and needed to take responsibility for his actions. He started attending therapy sessions and took up new hobbies, hoping to turn his life around.

After several years behind bars, Alex was finally released. He knew that he had a lot of work to do if he wanted to rebuild his life, but he was determined to make things right.

He started by reaching out to Jack and apologizing for what he had done. To his surprise, Jack was willing to forgive him and even offered him a job at his new company.

Over the years, Alex worked hard to regain Jack's trust and rebuild his reputation. He became known for his honesty and integrity and was eventually promoted to a high-level position within the company.

Although he had lost so much in his pursuit of revenge, Alex had learned an important lesson - that revenge only leads to more pain and suffering. Instead, he focused on making amends for his mistakes and building a better future for himself and those around him.

In the end, Alex realized that his success and happiness didn't come from revenge or material possessions but from his relationships with others and inner peace. He used his experiences to become a mentor to others who had been in his situation, and he devoted much of his time to volunteering and giving back to his community.

Looking back on his past, Alex realized that his quest for revenge had ultimately led him to a greater understanding of himself and his place in the world. While he couldn't change his mistakes, he could use them to help others and positively impact the world.

As he sat in his office overlooking the bustling city, Alex felt a sense of satisfaction and contentment that he had never experienced before. He knew that life would continue to bring challenges and setbacks, but he also knew he had the resilience and strength to overcome them.

With a smile, Alex picked up the phone and dialed his wife's number. As they chatted about their plans for the evening, he couldn't help but feel grateful for the second chance he had been given and for the people in his life who had stood by him through thick and thin.

For Alex, the greatest revenge had been finding happiness and fulfillment in a life well-lived.

The Abused Spouse

Lena had been married to her husband, Jack, for over a decade. Initially, their marriage had been full of love and hope for the future, but over time, Jack's behavior had become increasingly controlling and abusive. Lena had tried to leave him before, but he had always managed to track her down and bring her back.

One night, after a particularly violent argument, Lena knew she had to leave for good. She packed a bag and drove to a motel on the outskirts of town, hoping to start a new life away from Jack's abuse. But just a few days later, she received a message from him: he had hired a private investigator to find her.

Panicked and unsure of what to do, Lena confided in a friend who suggested a plan for revenge. They would set up a fake meeting with Jack, lure him to a secluded location, and record him confessing to his abusive behavior. Lena was hesitant at first, but as the messages from Jack became increasingly threatening, she knew it was her only option.

The day of the meeting arrived, and Lena was a bundle of nerves as she drove to the deserted parking lot where they had agreed to meet. Jack was already there, pacing back and forth with a scowl.

"What the hell is this, Lena?" he growled as she approached. "You think you can just run away from me? I'll always find you."

But Lena stood her ground, her heart pounding as she pulled out her phone and hit record. "I want to talk, Jack," she said, trying to keep her voice steady. "I want you to tell me the truth about what you've done to me."

Jack looked taken aback momentarily, his eyes flicking to the phone in Lena's hand. But then he sneered and lunged at her, trying to grab the phone. Lena stumbled back, heart racing, as she realized the plan might not work.

But just then, a police car pulled up, sirens blaring. Lena's friend had called in a tip about the meeting, and the police had been waiting nearby to intervene. They quickly apprehended Jack, who struggled and cursed as they handcuffed him.

In the following weeks, Lena worked closely with the police to build a case against Jack. She shared her story of abuse and provided evidence of his violent behavior. Ultimately, he was charged with domestic violence and sentenced to several years in prison.

For Lena, the road to recovery was a long and difficult one. She struggled with anxiety and PTSD, and it took time and therapy to heal from the trauma of her abusive marriage. But with the support of her friends and family, she was able to start a new life, free from the fear and violence that had once dominated her existence.

As she looked back on that fateful day in the parking lot, Lena knew that revenge had been a necessary step in her journey to healing. By exposing Jack's behavior and holding him accountable for his actions, she had taken back some measure of power and control over her life.

She waited a few moments to ensure he was gone and emerged from her hiding place, feeling a sense of relief. She knew she had to be careful now, as he would likely be searching for her, so she quickly went to a nearby coffee shop to think about her next move.

As she sat there sipping her coffee, she began formulating a plan. She knew that she needed to gather evidence of her husband's abusive behavior if she was to have any chance of escaping him for good. She decided to start documenting his actions and keeping a record of any abusive incidents.

Over the next few weeks, she carefully documented every instance of abuse, taking photos of any injuries and keeping a detailed record of what had happened. She also sought the help of a lawyer, who helped her to file for a restraining order and to begin divorce proceedings.

Her ex-husband was unhappy about this turn of events and began escalating his harassment. He would call her constantly, leave threatening messages, and even arrive at her workplace. She knew that she had to act fast to protect herself.

One day, she received a call from her ex-husband, asking to meet with her in a secluded spot. She knew this was her chance to expose him, so she agreed to the meeting.

When he arrived, she had set up a hidden camera and microphone to capture his confession. She confronted him about his abusive behavior and played back the recordings of his threatening messages to her. He became agitated and tried to grab the camera, but she managed to fend him off and escape.

She took the evidence to the police, who arrested and charged him with domestic violence. He was eventually found guilty and sentenced to a lengthy prison term. She felt a sense of closure and could finally move on with her life, free from his abuse and harassment.

It wasn't an easy journey for her, but she had finally escaped the clutches of her abusive ex-husband. She began to rebuild her life, seeking therapy to deal with the trauma she had experienced and focus.

She eventually met someone new, someone who treated her with respect and kindness. They fell in love and began to build a life together, one that was filled with joy and happiness.

She knew that the scars of her past would always be with her, but she also knew she was strong enough to overcome them. She became an advocate for victims of domestic violence, using her own story to inspire others to seek help and break free from their abusers.

Years later, she received a letter from her ex-husband, who was still serving his prison sentence. In it, he apologized for his actions and admitted that he had been wrong to treat her the way he had. She was surprised by the letter but felt a sense of closure, knowing he had finally taken responsibility for his actions.

She didn't forgive him, but she felt a sense of peace knowing that she had overcome the pain he had caused her. She continued to live her life with grace and resilience, a testament to the power of the human spirit to overcome even the darkest circumstances.

Looking back on her journey, she realized that it had all led her to this moment - that she could overcome any obstacle and had the strength to create the life she wanted.

She continued to advocate for victims of domestic violence, speaking out about her experiences and offering support to those who needed it. She also started a non-profit organization that provided resources and shelter to domestic violence victims, helping them escape from their abusers and start new lives.

She found purpose and fulfillment through her work and knew she was making a difference.

She also continued to nurture her relationship with her new partner, building a life filled with love, laughter, and joy. They traveled the world together, exploring new places and making memories that would last a lifetime.

As she reflected on her past, she realized that it had all been a part of her journey - a journey that had led her to a place of healing, growth, and happiness. She felt grateful for the lessons she had learned and the strength she had gained along the way.

As she looked toward the future, she knew that whatever challenges lay ahead, she would face them with courage, determination, and grace, for she was a survivor, a fighter, and a force to be reckoned with.

And so, she walked confidently into the future, knowing she had the power to shape her destiny. With each step she took, she felt a sense of freedom and strength, knowing she was no longer defined by her past but by the person she had become.

She smiled as she looked at the horizon, ready to embrace whatever lay ahead. She knew that life would bring challenges, but she was ready to face them head-on, armed with the knowledge that she could overcome anything.

Walking towards the setting sun, she felt a sense of peace and contentment wash over her. She felt truly alive for the first time in a long time, with a renewed sense of purpose and a joy that radiated from within.

She was a survivor, a warrior, and a woman who had found her way back to herself. And nothing, not even the darkest moments of her past, could ever take that away from her.

"Revenge may provide temporary satisfaction, but in the end, it only perpetuates a cycle of harm and consumes one with bitterness and resentment."

Ertugrul Odabasi

Milton Keynes UK
Ingram Content Group UK Ltd.
UKHW030724080824
446708UK00006B/45